The Bear
at
Cinnamon Lake

ISBN-13: 978-1-7377620-0
ISBN-10: 1-7377620-1-3

First printing, October 2021

Published by:

tm

ThomasMax Publishing
P.O. Box 250054
Atlanta, GA 30325

The Bear at Cinnamon Lake

Judith Barban

ThomasMax

Your Publisher
For The 21st Century

ACKNOLEDGMENTS

In making this book possible I have received support from so many people—friends, family, and professionals. I was encouraged and even challenged to begin writing *The Bear at Cinnamon Lake* by my good friend and fellow writer William Moore, author of the heart-warming novel, *A Teacher's Tears*, a book that has touched so many lives. As the work progressed, I came to depend on my amazing nephew, Dr. Alan Calder, professor of Astrophysics at SUNY Stony Brook, for his expertise in the fields of auto mechanics and bow hunting.

A huge thank-you to my circle of readers whose enthusiasm gave me the encouragement to follow through with the project. And, of course, primary among those readers was my husband Eugene whose comments and suggestions proved invaluable.

I owe a debt of gratitude to Canadian lodge owners, outfitters, and guides from whom I have learned so much about the wilderness, its flora and fauna. More importantly, they demonstrate how to love, respect, and protect pristine nature. I am especially appreciative of the help received from Kevin Walsten of Walsten Outposts (Ontario) and Jodi and Trevor Dick of Bolton Lake Lodge (Manitoba).

Above all, I want to thank my indefatigable publisher/editor Lee Clevenger of ThomasMax Publishing for his faith in my work, for his always spot-on judgment, for his creative ideas, and for his friendship through the years. Lee, you are the best!

Judith Barban

FOREWORD

The Bear at Cinnamon Lake is the third book in my Poplar River trilogy. While all three are works of fiction, each was inspired by actual events. *Poplar River*, the first in the group, came as the results of many years fishing with my husband Gene at remote, solitary outposts in the Canadian wilderness. Most of the adventures recorded in the book really happened to us, one or two were related by other fishermen in the cabin logbook, some were recounted to us by our outfitter. The story is told through the eyes of a young concert pianist from Springhill, South Carolina. She and her husband, an English professor at the local college, spend their honeymoon at Poplar River outpost, a gift from her husband's cousin. There Karen feels a deep connection to pristine Nature and its flora and fauna and looks forward to returning the same week each year. She is drawn to a bald eagle, a beaver, a moose, a colony of mice, and a loon. She has a strange experience with a bear. Her path crosses that of an Ojibwe living in the wilderness who inspires her to learn about indigenous peoples' culture. Each week the adventure is told first from Karen's point of view then from that of the particular animal. At home Karen experiences the tragedy of her husband's suicide and the triumph of her overwhelmingly successful concert career. She learns to cope with it all when she returns to Poplar River and begins a new life. The book was years in the making due to the months of research on animals and vegetation of the boreal forest and on Ojibwe traditions. But it all paid off: the book won the coveted "You Are Published" prize sponsored by the Southeastern Writers' Association and offered by ThomasMax Publishers.

Meredith's Wolf drew inspiration from the young son of Dick Hebel, owner of Cobham River Lodge and Outposts. At the wilderness lodge in northeastern Manitoba, the boy found an abandoned wolf pup and raised it to adulthood. So does my character Meredith, Karen's daughter. As she approaches her fifteenth birthday her stepfather urges her to release the now-grown wolf back into the wild. She is reluctant, so he promises to teach her to fly the seaplane if she returns the wolf. She agrees. She earns her pilot's license and masters the art of flying and docking single-handedly. She and her stepfather fly north to a remote area and release the wolf. But Meredith is stubborn. During her mother's and stepfather's absence from the lodge she flies up to see her wolf. She is forced to land in a storm and gets lost in the wilderness—an easy thing to do. Mark, a young Ojibwe, grandson of the one her mother met, rescues her and an innocent romantic relationship is formed. He escorts her to reunite with "Wolfie." But the two are captured by poachers who threaten their lives. Meanwhile a pregnant Karen and her husband are frantically searching. The non-stop adventure is told by Meredith, Karen, and, of course, Wolfie. This book has brought me a number of faithful and enthusiastic followers.

The Bear at Cinnamon Lake was inspired by the real-life rescue of a victim of a bear mauling by my friend and favorite outfitter Kevin Walsten. Kevin is one of Canada's finest outfitters and an excellent bush pilot. He checks on his outposts frequently. During one flight check he found the fisherman in serious condition and flew him to a hospital. In essence, he saved the man's life. In the novel, Meredith becomes the rescuer. The bear attack is the point of departure for two adventure-filled wilderness journeys—that of a man and that of the bear. For these journeys I called upon all my experiences in camps and outposts in wilderness of Manitoba and Ontario. In writing this book I delighted in being able to take the two journeys with man and beast and so will the reader. I enjoyed spending imaginative time as well as real time in the town of Kenora, Ontario, a quaint city on the northern shore of Lake of the Woods. At one point I considered retiring there. But I could not pull up my Southern roots. Now come with me to the far north where the green canopy of the boreal forest and all its marvelous creatures await!

To all Canadians whose love, respect, and protection of their country's boreal forest have preserved an amazingly pristine wilderness for everyone to experience and enjoy.

Thank you!

OTHER BOOKS BY JUDITH BARBAN FROM THOMASMAX PUBLISHING

Poplar River

Judith Barban

Karen Kingsley and her husband have been given a honeymoon trip to Poplar River in the Canadian wilderness by her husband's cousin, Bobby. Karen immediately finds herself at home in the wild and develops into an expert fisherwoman who looks forward to returning to Poplar River. But all is not well with Karen, despite the birth of a daughter and musical skills that bring her more offers than she can accept. She loses twin sons, then finds her husband mysteriously depressed. In a sort-of reverse *Dr. Doolittle*, Karen's encounters with the animals of Poplar River are first told through her eyes, then through the eyes of the animals who tell their sides of the stories.

Meredith's Wolf

Judith Barban

When Meredith Marsten's floatplane loses power in a storm, the 16-year-old Canadian bush pilot is forced to land on an unknown lake isolated in the wilderness of northern Manitoba, Canada. Realizing that the lake is the very one where she and her step-father had released her now-grown wolf pup back into the wild, Meredith embarks on a quest to reunite with her beloved "Wolfie." Thus she begins a suspenseful journey through the ristine boreal forest, a journey full of encounters with the drama of nature, animals, humans, and her own surprising destiny. Second book in the *Poplar River* trilogy.

CROWN JEWELS

poetry by
Judith Barban

Illustrated by Rosemary C. Gray

Award-winning novelist Judith Barban brings together this collection of poetic gemstones that sparkle with wit, pathos, candor and artful ingenuity. With illustrations by Rosemary C. Gray

Chapter One
The Attack

"Okay, you guys. Up and at 'em! Coffee's perking!" Terrence stood at the door of Billy's and Jake's bunk room. Jake groaned. Billy pulled the sleeping bag over his head and turned toward the wall.

"You both promised. Portage to Wheeler Lake today. Our last chance for a trophy walleye. Hey, I think coffee's ready." He turned back toward the central room of the two-bedroom cabin.

Billy poked his head out slowly. He could smell the steaming brew but turtled his head back in. *We did promise him. Rather sleep in. Shouldn't have had that bourbon on top of the beers.*

"Come on, Billy. We are committed to this. I don't know why he's so fixed on fishing another lake."

Billy rolled over. Jake sat on the side of his cot, a little haggard, running his hands through his mussed-up hair.

With a sigh of resignation Billy unzipped his sleeping bag and got to his feet.

"I don't either. With the fishing so good in Cinnamon. My arms are sore from pulling in a bunch of hefty northern pike yesterday."

"Yeah. You did haul in a few. I was pretty lucky too."

Billy grabbed his jeans off a wall hook, hopped on first one foot then the other to get them on, donned a flannel shirt and joined Terry at the coffee pot.

"Where's Jake?"

"He's coming. We're all going to Wheeler Lake right after you whip up some eggs and bacon."

"You got it." Terrence hadn't proven to be much of a fisherman, but his chef skills were a welcome surprise.

With breakfast over and dishes washed, the men selected rods and reels for the day. After some discussion of which reel was best for walleye fishing and which for pike, they came to a mutual agreement: each would carry a spinning reel and lighter rod for walleye, a bait-casting reel and heavier rod for the big northern pike. Jake decided to take a backpack with a few snacks, a first aid kit, a thermos of water, and a roll of toilet paper.

"You never know when nature calls," he needlessly explained.

"You got any insect spray? The black flies are eating me alive," Billy said.

"I noticed the bites when you were getting dressed. I don't have any spray myself. Do you, Terry?"

"No, sorry. But there's a plastic bottle filled with something that smells like insect repellent." Terrence opened a cabinet and handed the bottle to Billy.

"I'll give it a try." Billy rubbed the liquid onto his arms, face, neck, and into his hair.

Jake backed up. "Whoa!! Keep your distance, man! That stuff is nasty!"

"Yeah, it is. But it's better than itching, stinging bites from those pestiferous bugs." Wearing hiking boots and each carrying a tackle box and two rods loaded with reels, the three men filed out the front door. Although it was early, the sun was already high and warm but could barely penetrate the thick foliage of the covered taiga forest. A light breeze from Cinnamon Lake still carried a bit of morning chill. Directly behind the cabin Billy found the marked tree that indicated entrance to the portage route.

Jake did an about face. "Hold up, guys. I forgot my backpack."

"Be sure to close the door. Keep the critters out." Billy felt he should be in charge of the expedition since he was the organizer of this fishing trip. He had more experience fishing in Canada that either of the others. He had tried to make the guys better fishermen and better outdoorsmen. Jake had really improved his fishing skills and seemed to really get into it. Terrence not so much. That's what made it hard to understand his enthusiasm for the portage to Wheeler Lake.

Jake caught up with Billy and Terrence. "I strapped on my filet knife so we can carve up the fish before we head back."

"That's thinking ahead, my man. Presuming we catch enough walleye for dinner." Billy forged on, swatting at flies as he went. "I don't think this stuff is working." Despite blood-sucking insects' delight in his tender skin, Billy loved the outdoors, especially the Canadian wilderness—or "bush," as they call it. He tried to spend a week each summer fishing at an outpost. This year he selected Cinnamon Lake, an outpost of Baldwin Lake Lodge. Minimum of three guests, the brochure said. He could count on Jake, but finding a third party wasn't easy. A friend-of-a-friend put him in touch with Terrence:

"I'm really excited about going with you guys and having a little outdoor adventure. Love fishing," he said on the phone. Billy thought he would work out, and so far he had.

The path was well delineated so the hike was easy. Not long into the trek Billy started noticing long strands of black fur caught on some of the waist-level bushes and tree trunks. He said nothing about it but felt the hair on the back of his neck stand up.

The three men trudged on in silence, pausing once for a sip of water from Jake's thermos.

"I think I caught a glimpse of the lake," Terrence said. He pushed past Billy and hurried ahead. "Oh, yeah. It's not far," he called back.

Billy shook his head. *Why is he so eager to get there? He hasn't shown much enthusiasm about fishing on Cinnamon, or fishing, period.*

A sound of something moving in the underbrush just off the path. Billy stopped, put down his tackle box, and listened. Some kind of heavy animal was moving through the bush. Coming this way. Very close. Billy froze. Heart pumping, breath rapid. Out of nowhere there stood a large black bear on the path between him and Terrence. The bear looked straight at Billy, making vocalizations and turning his head from side to side, foam forming around its mouth. Lips curled back. Billy stared at the huge symmetrical fangs.

"Give me your filet knife belt, Jake. Leave your rods and tackle and slowly go into the bush. Find a tree you can climb." Billy spoke slowly and quietly, without taking his eyes off the bear while he strapped on the knife from Jake. With rods in one hand and knife in the other Billy raised his arms and waved them in an attempt to intimidate the bear the bear.

"Yo-o-o-o-, Bear! Get away. Go. Ho-o-o-o-o!" He jumped up and down and made loud noises he hoped sounded menacing to the animal.

In vain. The bear stood up, showing its preponderant size and making more frightening sounds than any human could utter.

Everything went into slow motion. Billy knew that as soon as the bear's front paws met the ground again, it would charge him. And it did. Billy could feel the ground shake with every loping stride. *If I can stick the knife in one of its eyes, that will stop him.* In one lunge toward the charging bear Billy struck with the knife. But he missed and cut the animal's cheek slightly below the left eye. The bear howled in pain, slowing for a moment. Infuriated, the bear renewed the charge with more determination.

The cabin. If I can make it there I'll be safe. In spite of knowing that running from a bear is the wrong thing to do, Billy obeyed a primal instinct for survival and started running back toward the cabin.

He didn't run for long. He heard the bear's forceful breathing closing in, could smell its foul breath. The next second he felt the power of the bear's paws landing on his back and pushing him to the ground. Billy let go of the bloody knife and clasped his hands over the back of his head. *Got to protect my brain.*

A searing pain in his right shoulder. The bear held it in its mouth, sinking his teeth deep into the flesh and bone. When it released its grip on Billy's shoulder, it started clawing at his back and neck.

Billy screamed—a primal scream that humans can make only when terrorized. *No! Not my spinal cord!*

Saliva from the bear's mouth and blood from the facial cut dripped onto Billy's lacerated back. Its breath was hot and moist. Billy felt the bear's teeth sinking into his flesh. *Oh, God, no! Don't let him eat me!* Images of Billy's family flashed through his mind. His wife, Lacey, the love of his life and mother of his beautiful four-year-old son. His own mother and father, still alive, still in good health. They gave him everything. His sister Angie, his confidant, with her gorgeous brown eyes. He may never see them again. *Dear God, help me! Help me now!*

With both forepaws still on its victim's back, the bear began to lick Billy's arms, neck and hair. *Why is he doing that? At least he's not biting or clawing anymore.*

The licking stopped. Billy could feel the bear's paws and forearms pouncing up and down on his back like a kid on a trampoline. Each time the weight came down on his back it compressed Billy's chest and stopped his breathing. When he had enough of pounding, the bear stood over its victim sniffing and snorting. It swatted at Billy's body a few times and made grunting noises.

Play dead, Billy remembered reading. He did, for what seemed an eternity. The bear walked away, then returned, pounced a few more times, snorted and growled. Billy didn't move and kept his breathing quiet and to a minimum. The bear set a pattern of turning away then coming back to sniff and paw its victim. Billy waited until he felt sure the bear had gone for good. He found the knife and tried to get to his feet but could not stand up straight. Hunched over, with blood pouring down his right arm, he would take a few steps and fall.

Must get to the cabin and call for help. Or else I won't make it. Bear may be after Jake or Terry.

The forest seemed endless, enormous. Several times he thought he heard the bear lumbering toward him again, thought he could hear the snorting. Each time he went into survival position face down, hands locked over his head. Somehow he got off the path. Brambles and shrubs tore at his clothing and face and made the going even more difficult, but it didn't matter. He pressed on crawling on his belly until he could see the cabin through the leaves. His strength completely failed. He could only propel his body forward with his left forearm. He made it beyond the outhouse. Only a few steps from the side door of the cabin, Billy passed out.

Chapter Two
The Victim

Meredith had a bad feeling as the Cessna floatplane lifted off the waters of Baldwin Lake. The three men fishing for the week at Cinnamon Lake outpost were not scheduled to be picked up until tomorrow. But for three days there had been no contact with base lodge via satellite phone. No response at six am this morning when she tried to reach them. Rarely do fishermen go out before then, especially after enjoying a night of beer drinking and bragging. And these guys had brought in enough brew to make each of their seven evenings a fourth-of-July bash and each morning slow-to-go. Instinct told her something was wrong. Before she headed to the floatplane dock, she found her husband in the lodge office preparing final bills for the lodge and outpost guests flying back to Winnipeg in the morning.

"Mark, I'm going up to check on the guys at Cinnamon."

Her husband turned from the computer. "Why is that?"

"I don't know. Just a gut feeling they may be in trouble. No one answered when I called really early this morning to tell them what time I would be in tomorrow."

"Probably out fishing, taking full advantage of their last day."

"You're probably right, but still . . . . " Meredith had learned to obey her instincts.

The nearer she flew to the cabin at Cinnamon, the more uneasy she became. The weather was good—light winds in a favorable direction, smooth water surface. Tangerine clouds lingered from the early August sunrise. When the jigsaw-puzzle shape of Cinnamon came into view, Meredith started a direct descent toward the water. On the far side of the lake she could see the windows of the log cabin peering out through poplars and jack pines. Once the pontoons made contact and the plane leveled off, she cut the engine. Her step-father, lodge owner and bush pilot *par excellence*, had taught her how to allow the plane to drift to the dock then step down the horizontal bars across the struts and jump onto the dock, grab the mooring ropes—wing first then tail—and tie up. It was an amazing one-man operation that she had marveled at since childhood. Piece of cake for her now. She knew how proud Bobby was of his step-daughter's ability to negotiate this single-handed maneuver.

After the whirring din of the plane's engine, Meredith welcomed the hushed softness of wilderness sounds. The delicate rustle of poplar leaves responding to gentle wind gusts, the hopping of gray jays from limb to limb, the scratching of boreal chickadees searching for a meal from the forest floor, the gentle lap-lap of lake water against the shore. She glanced around. Two boats moored, one on each side of the dock.

So they're not out fishing on Cinnamon. Maybe they took the short portage over to Wheeler Lake.

A dirt path led from the dock straight to the front deck of the cabin. The deck wrapped around three sides and provided the perfect spot for evening beer-drinking and talk of the days' fishing exploits. Strange. The front door was wide open. An invitation to mosquitoes, black flies, and larger wild creatures. The guys should know better.

No one in the central room. The table was cluttered with fishing lure, a lake map, a compass, and two spinning reels evidently rejected for today's outing. Kitchen trash can full of empty, crushed beer cans, the two bunk beds in one bedroom scattered with T-shirts, jackets, jeans. Socks and underwear tossed on the floor. Men's toiletries on the basin in the shower room. Nothing unusual.

But she couldn't shake the eerie feeling.

A slapping noise. Then a dragging sound. Meredith glanced out the double front window. Just the Cessna. Lake still calm. She decided to check the outhouse. Taking the side door onto the deck she started down the steps but stopped short. Her throat locked up. Not far from the steps, on the path to the latrine, lay a man face down. The back of his clothing was shredded and soaked in blood. He reached one hand forward and lifted his face to her.

"Bear. Help me!"

His breath came in ragged gasps. His eyes were completely dilated.

Meredith had no time to think. She had to act quickly or the man would die. He was obviously in shock. A few quick strides to reach him. She stooped down, took the extended arm and put it around her shoulder.

"Can you get to your feet?"

"Don't know."

"Try. I'll help you."

Pulling on his torso with the other arm she managed to get the man upright. He would take a few steps then collapse his weight on her. A couple of times they both went down and had to begin the whole process again. She practically had to drag him down the front path and out onto the dock, all the while glancing around for any sign of a bear made hungry by the taste of human blood. Where were his buddies? Why was he alone? Where did he meet up with a bear? Why did the bear attack? No way she could get answers now. Interrogation would have to wait.

It took superhuman strength to push him up the rungs into the pilot's seat then over to the copilot's.

"I've got to do this," Meredith kept telling herself. "Please, God, give me strength. Please don't let this man die on me."

Once at the controls, she radioed Mark.

"Call immediately for a medivac copter. I'm bringing in a victim of a bear attack. It's bad. Be there in twenty minutes."

She looked at the passenger. His head had fallen to one side and his eyes were closed.

"Don't you dare pass out on me. Can you hear me? Wake up! Stay with me! You'll have medical help in just a few minutes, you hear?"

She kept directing the same command to him throughout the short flight.

"Stay with me now*!" I can't let this guy lose consciousness.*

When she saw no evidence of a response, she would reach over and shake his shoulder. Groanings were a good sign, though he was now incapable of words. He looked to be in his early fifties, medium build, but muscular. A week's growth of beard, straight reddish-blond hair, the back of it caked with blood. Most of the lodge and outpost guests were returnees year after year, but he was one of three new fishermen this week. Their names were listed at the lodge but she had been in email correspondence with only one of them. Billy something. He had given her the names of the other two in his group for the fishing licenses. But she hadn't had time to get to know or recognize them individually.

"At least his chest and abdomen seem okay. Thank God for that."

The claw and teeth damage was mainly to the back and neck. She worried about the condition of his spine and kidneys. Never before had a guest been attacked by a bear.

"When you're in the wilderness, wild animals, especially bears, are always a danger, Mister . . .sorry I don't know your name. You always have to be on your guard," she told her uncomprehending passenger. "I guess it's a little late for that advice."

The flight back to Baldwin seemed an eternity. Gurgling sounds came from the victim, but Meredith had to focus on the landing. She pulled up to the dock, copilot side. Bobby, her husband Mark, and two of the lodge guides were there waiting with something that resembled a homemade stretcher.

"One of the lodge guests is an orthopedic surgeon. He'll administer first aid and do what he can until SAR gets here. They're sending the wheeled Otter to fly him directly to Winnipeg. Then a helicopter will airlift him to the hospital." Bobby's rapid, short sentences somewhat alleviated Meredith's anxiety until she looked down at her blood-smeared jacket and jeans. Suddenly she felt sick, her legs so weak she had to sit down on the dock.

Why did this have to happen now? Just when Mark and I are learning to manage the lodge and outposts. She took several deep breaths. *Our baptism by fire I guess. Thank God Bobby and Karen are here training us. But they have never had to deal with a bear attack. And thank God I went up there today. The man would have died. What about the others? Could the bear have attacked more than one? Killed one? Where were the other two guys? What if there are more victims at Cinnamon? Someone must go back to find them!*

The urgency of the thought got her to her feet. She climbed up the rungs of the Cessna.

"Wait, Mer! Are you crazy? You can't go back up there alone!" Mark called out as he hurried toward the dock, a rifle hanging on one shoulder. Meredith was already in the pilot's seat ready for take-off. Mark slid into the cockpit beside her. "We've got to find and kill that bear before he gets either of the others – if it's not already too late!"

Once they reached altitude Mark continued. "Did you think you could rescue two guys and kill the marauding bear with no weapon?"

"There's a crossbow in the back of the plane. I'm pretty good with it."

"Not good enough."

That was the extent of their conversation until they reached the cabin. The plane was moored in seconds then both of them re-checked the interior of the cabin, hoping to see the two men safe and sound, but doubtless terrified.

"It's just like I found it," Meredith said.

"Okay. Listen. You take this." Mark pulled a can of bear spray out of his hoodie pocket. "We need to walk all the way around the cabin, then try to determine where the guy or the bear came out of the bush. Stay right with me."

"Don't worry, you've got the gun."

The area around the cabin was rife with blueberry bushes. Meredith noticed that the only fruit left was near the top beyond the reach of a standing bear. They searched the front, back, and opposite side of the house without noticing anything unusual.

"Show me exactly where you found the man lying."

Meredith led him to the spot. "The attack obviously didn't occur here. Judging from the trail of blood, he must have dragged himself from the woods." She noticed Mark squinting his eyes in that first-nations style when scrutinizing and thinking. He took a few steps, squatted down and picked up something then held it out for her to see.

"A filet knife?" she questioned.

"Yes, And a bloody one."

"I didn't see that before"

"Probably because it was under his body."

"Is it human blood or bear blood?"

"Good question. I saw that he was wearing a leather filet-knife holster when we brought him up to the lodge. It was empty."

"Maybe he used it to try to defend himself."

"Could be. But we don't have time to theorize about what happened. Let's follow the trail left by his body and blood. It may lead us to the other two guys."

"Or the bear."

"Take this." Mark handed her the filet knife.

Meredith glanced at the skinny blade. *As if this little thing would have a chance against a wounded, angry bear.* She reasoned with herself as they traced the body marks and blood smears. *I have had encounters with bears before. They have never made any attempt to harm me.* Once she and Mark were having a meal at one of Baldwin Lake shore lunch spots when Mark looked up from his plate, his gaze just behind Meredith. He said one word, "Bear!" She turned around to find a huge black bear staring not at her, but at their plates of fried walleye nuggets. Her first instinct was to run to the boat. Instead both she and Mark stood up on the picnic table benches, waved their arms above their heads and yelled as loud as they could. The bear turned and lumbered back into the bush. And there were other episodes. *But this bear has tasted human blood and flesh, found it delicious, and would like to enjoy some more.*

The blood trail led toward the woods near the latrine. Mark pointed to some dark stains low on a serviceberry shrub with broken branches.

"Here's where he came out."

Meredith nodded, not wanting to speak for fear of alerting the bear. But of course if it were still nearby it had already smelled and heard them.

Mark cupped his hands around his mouth and called out "Anyone there? We're here to help! The cabin is safe now. We have weapons! Let me know if you are out there!" Megaphone style, Mark reiterated the message in several directions, each time pausing for a response.

He didn't seem to share her feelings about silence. But we really were here to help. Not just to keep ourselves alive. Meredith shuddered and felt a little queasy. Why was she always trying to prove herself to Mark? Since the day he found her lost in the wilderness, crying like a helpless goat, she has felt a constant need to show her tough mettle. Well, the current circumstances were giving her the perfect opportunity to do just that. The thought made her stand tall and tune acute ears to any kind of sound from the woods.

"I think I heard something, Mark! Someone calling 'I'm here!'"

"Which direction?"

Meredith pointed a little to the right in the direction of the Ontario border. "I think from over there. It was real faint."

The megaphone again. "Say again louder! Keep calling until we find you!"

Mark slid the rifle off his shoulder and positioned it. "Stay as close to me as possible. And keep listening."

With the bear spray in a pocket and the filet knife in her right hand, she used her free hand to maneuver through the underbrush. Courage and determination began to build and give her strength. Fear subsided.

"Over here!" The call was louder. They were heading in the right direction.

"I heard him," Mark said and picked up the pace. The fisherman's voice sounded strong, so he was probably not hurt, at least not like his colleague, Meredith told herself.

They were now on the portage path to Wheeler Lake which made the going easier and faster.

"Up here!" the voice cried.

And there he was, high in a poplar, clinging to the narrow tree trunk with one arm and waving to them with the other.

"I can't get down!!"

"I'm coming up to help you, but first throw down your backpack. It'll make things easier." Mark was at the base of the tree looking up at the man. He handed the rifle to Meredith, shimmied up to the lowest branch, and began the ascent. Meredith grabbed the backpack and slung it over her shoulder but kept a firm grip on the weapon.

Just to reassure herself, she glanced 180 degrees to the left and 180 degrees to the right. The only sound was Mark giving limb-by-limb directions to the camper. It seemed to take forever, but they finally made it down. Mark had to steady the man who was shaky and weak from the ordeal. He tried to speak. Words formed on his lips but he hadn't the force to project them.

"It's okay, buddy. You're safe now. You can relate the whole story after we get you back to the cabin." He motioned for Meredith to pass the rifle. "My wife will help you. Hang on to her."

Meredith put the backpack on properly and checked to make sure the bear spray was still in her pocket. Wrapping one arm around the camper's torso, she held on to the knife with the other. *It will be slow going getting back.*

Once inside, Meredith seated the guy and dropped the backpack. "I'll get you some water," she offered, "or maybe you'd rather have a beer?"

"No, water's fine."

"I'm sorry. I don't remember your name. You're new this year."

"Jake Hammergren." First time for the three of us." He gulped down the water she handed him, swiped the back of his hand across his mouth, and let out a heavy sigh of relief.

"Did you see the attack?"

"Not really. Billy lit out for the cabin and the bear took after him. I was already mostly up the tree."

"You're lucky the bear decided to go after . . . Billy. Black bears are excellent climbers. He could have easily pulled you out of that poplar." Mark warned. "What happened to the third fellow?"

"I have no idea."

Meredith and Mark exchanged *what do we do now?* glances.

* * *

They were late closing up the lodge. Word about the bear victim had spread among the twenty-four guests in the lodge cabins. More guests than usual at the bar, more alcohol sold, more late-nighters.

"Mark, I'll never sleep tonight. Only three months into our management of the lodge and look what we're dealing with." Meredith closed the door to their rear apartment and began undressing.

"Think this way," Mark advised. "Only three months ago we had a fantastic wedding. When I'm worried and can't sleep, I think about how beautiful you looked that day and I go to sleep happy."

"Okay. I'll try your method of sleep inducement." She slipped into bed, pulled up the duvet against the cool Canadian night, and began to remember that most important day in her life.

Chapter Three
The Wedding

"Oh, Nakomis!! They are beautiful! They are perfect!" Meredith took the white Ojibwe wedding moccasins out of the box and held one in each hand. "I love the pink rose in the beaded vamp!" She set one down and caressed the other. "They are so soft. Is it deerskin?"

"Elk. I was able to get some elk hide from a Red Lake tribe member who makes moccasins. It will hold up better than deer. But I wasn't sure what color you would want the rose—red, blue, pink, or yellow—so I asked Mark. He chose pink."

"It's what I would have chosen, too." She put both shoes back into the box and smiled at her grandmother-in-law. "How can I ever thank you?"

"Agreeing to have an Ojibwe ceremony is thanks enough. The whole clan is excited. We're selecting foods, flowers, and musicians who will play native music on traditional instruments as you requested."

"Have you seen my dress?"

"No, I haven't. But I am dying to!" Nakomis clasped her hands together and brought them up to her chest. Her eyes and smile spoke for her heart. Despite her graying hair and facial wrinkles, she had an aura of eternal youth. Meredith had come to adore Mark's grandmother.

"Well, let me go get it for you. You know, Mama has always wanted to help me pick out my dress, so we did an internet search for Native American wedding clothes. Finally spotted the right dress. It arrived just last week."

She left Nakomis in the living room of her parents' quaint little Winnipeg home and hurried upstairs. She was over-the-moon about this light-weight deerskin dress. White, of course, with ragland sleeves to the elbow from which fringe of the same material hung to the mid-calf hem. The sleeves and bodice were framed with a wide band of dark grosgrain ribbon embroidered with green leaves and tiny purple flowers. Beaded pink roses dotted the neck and chest.

"See how the shoes perfectly match the dress." Meredith held the garment up against her body for Nakomis to see.

Grandmother stood to better admire the wedding dress. She ran her fingertips over the beaded roses and gently rubbed the material of the slightly-flared skirt.

"It's fine quality and handsome work. You will be the most beautiful bride ever!" She opened her arms and hugged Meredith, dress and all. "My friends will be jealous that I have already seen THE wedding dress. I can't wait to tell them. You know we haven't had a traditional wedding in a long time. The last bride wanted nothing to do with our rituals. She and her boyfriend slipped off to a Justice of the Peace. We were all so disappointed." She gathered up her purse and jacket and headed for the front door. "Well, I'm off. It's only a week away!"

When the door closed, Meredith wrapped her arms around the dress and held it close.

"Oh. Mark! We've waited so long for this!!" She shut her eyes and envisioned her first encounter with Mark in the wilderness, his birch-bark wigwam and bearskin bed where she spent the night while Mark slept outdoors. She had felt so safe, so confident that Mark would lead her to the wolf she had raised then released back into the wild. She relived the next night on the tarp under the stars listening to the howling wolfpack, her reunion with Wolfie, and then the kiss, the kiss that said so much about their future. She opened her eyes. "Five years ago. And now it's all coming to pass," she whispered.

The five years had not been slack. Both completed university degrees—Mark a Master's in Forestry and Meredith a Bachelor's in Wildlife Management. Both were on the job market. There had been a few employment offers, but not what either wanted.

"The right one will come along for each of us. Let's not be in a hurry for anything except to be together forever," she had said. And the wedding plans began.

"I want to combine my two worlds, Mark. A traditional Ojibwe ceremony but with a Presbyterian minister hearing our vows and pronouncing us man and wife. Will you be okay with the idea of a hybrid wedding?" Meredith saw little difference between Native American and Christian beliefs. With both in her mind and spirit, she seemed to understand the universe and its Creator. She felt complete, for the one complemented the other. The pieces just fit together.

"I would be okay with a polar bear doing the rites along with a mariachi band providing music, if that's what would make you happy and get us hitched!"

"And you're sure you're okay with me retaining my alliterative last name?"

"I *love* your alliterative name, Meredith Marsten."

"Well, that was easy. Keep that attitude and all will go extremely well I promise. Seriously, though, I need some help planning the ceremony. I've researched a little, but I still feel I don't know enough to pull it off without making mistakes. And I want it to be right."

"I know just the person you need. My maternal grandmother. Her name is Betty, but she wants to be called Nakomis by younger members of the family. She still lives on the rez sticking to tradition as much as possible, says she'll never leave. She knows all about the old ways. She's getting up in years but still has plenty of spitfire in her! She'll enlist the whole tribe to help."

"Can you put me in touch with her?"

"Will do."

* * *

"Mama, please keep trying. I really want my hair up in a French twist."

"Curly hair is not easy to control, you know. Bear with me. I have an idea." Karen gathered her daughter's hair into an upsweep in the back, pinned it, but allowed a bouquet of tawny curls to fall over the clasp. She pulled down a strand of soft wispy curls to hang in front of each ear. "There. What do you think?" Meredith took the hand mirror and swiveled around to see the side and back of her head in the dresser mirror.

"It's great, Mama! It's me. You always find a solution to all my problems!"

"After today you're on your own. A married woman responsible for everything in her life."

"Oh, don't say that! I'll never stop needing you." Meredith started to get up, eager to get the ceremony going.

"Wait. Don't forget your head feathers." Karen slid a black headband under the spray of curls and settled it on the girl's forehead. She nestled two eagle feathers into the band through the hair in the back so that they stood up like a victory sign.

"Now get up and let me see the complete outfit." She took a deep breath. "You look like a real Ojibwe bride."

"Yeah. Sure. With this hair?"

"You know, Sweetie, I've been thinking. Tom, Mark's grandfather, rescued your father and me when we were lost in the forest of Poplar River years ago. And Mark rescued you when you were also lost in the forest. So you are joining a family of rescuers."

"But, Mama, I'm a rescuer, too. I rescued a wolf."

Karen threw an arm around her daughter and drew her close. "You certainly did!"

The dressing room door opened admitting Meredith's aunt Katherine, Karen's sister, and an adorable five-year-old girl with dark curly hair wearing a little white deerskin dress that matched Meredith's minus the long fringe.

"My flower girl!" Meredith stooped to embrace her young sister. "You look gorgeous! You're not nervous are you, Jen?"

"A little. I hope I don't fall down."

"Don't be silly! You'll be fine. The star of the show."

Jenny giggled. "No, you are!"

Her mother and aunt had opted for pastel spring suits. Bobby would walk her to the front arbor where the black-robed Presbyterian minister, Tom as elder of the tribe, and the groom would be standing. Bobby, Tom, and Mark would wear the traditional black pants, black sash, and white ribbon shirts with a yellow, red, and black ribbon band sewn across the back, the chest and down each side of the front.

Sounds of the traditional flute a bec could be heard set against the persistent beat of the hand drum. Meredith turned to have one last look at her outfit. She closed her eyes and took a deep breath. "Great Spirit, God of All Creation, please be with us today," she said as a whispered prayer. The ladies left the dressing room, Jenny leading the way.

The women stepped out of the old restored farmhouse that served as a dressing area for the bride, and into a dazzling sunlit garden set up with white covered chairs on each side of a flat stone walkway to the front where the men stood under a trellis made of natural birch tree logs through which white voile and greenery intertwined. Karen and Meredith had spent weeks searching out the perfect outdoor venue. They wandered through all the parks and green spaces in Winnipeg. Meredith had begun to despair of ever finding the right spot until she discovered Green Gardens on the south side of the city. Just the right size, the wooden arbor with a stone fountain on one side and a fire pit on the other was perfect. Both mother and daughter had fervently prayed for sunshine on the chosen day. Meredith held her face up to the sun, closed her eyes for a moment and silently expressed her thanks to God.

After Katherine and Karen were escorted and seated, Jenny happily began spreading the contents of her basket creating a colorful path for the bride: wild blue flax, oxeye daisies, white bunch berry flowers, and yellow hawk's beard. The high-pitched sound of the eagle whistle signaled the arrival of the bride. Nakomis had to get special permission to use the tiny sacred flute-whistle in the ceremony. Now Bobby was at Meredith's side. She took his arm and they moved down the stone path to the arbor, two non-native Canadians and certainly two non-indigenous people dressed in Ojibwe attire, walking to tribal flute and drum music.

"What am I doing, Bobby? I feel foolish," she whispered.

"You're getting married."

Well, I do have Canadian and American citizenship. And Mark is Ojibwe. So it's OK.

That's all she had time to think. Bobby positioned her beside Mark then sat down next to Karen. A cool breeze refreshed her cheeks and helped her focus on the moment. She smiled at Mark whose eyes spoke volumes of joy. The minister began.

"Beloved, we are gathered . . . ," He had them hold hands, asked if each would take the other as husband and wife, and directed the exchange of rings. Meredith had not seen the ring Mark picked out until now. She had requested a medium gold and silver band engraved with flora and fauna of the wilderness. She caught her breath. It was even more beautiful than she had imagined. Mark wanted a simple gold band with the words "waterfall" and "mni-ha-ha" inscribed on the inner surface in English and in Anishinabe to commemorate their meeting in the forest and the waterfall where she bathed that day. It became her Ojibwe name.

"The elder of the tribe will hear your vows." The minister stepped aside and Tom took his place in front of the couple.

"We will now observe the Rite of Seven Steps. Meredith and Mark, see the semicircle of seven stones before you. Stones represent strength so that the solidity of the oaths that you make on each will endure. Take this eagle feather in your left hand, place a foot on each stone one at a time and declare your intentions as man and wife. When you have completed the semicircle, you will recite a prayer to the Great Spirit, your Creator. Then, after the blanket exchange the minister and I will offer a blessing upon you."

Each took the feather and stepped to the first stone:

"Let us take the first step to provide for our household a nourishing and pure diet, avoiding those foods injurious to healthy living." Meredith spoke.

"Let us take the second step to develop physical, mental and spiritual powers." Mark spoke.

"Let us take the third step to increase our wealth by righteous means and proper use."
Meredith spoke.

"Let us take the fourth step to acquire knowledge, happiness, and harmony by mutual love and trust." Mark.

"Let us take the fifth step so that we may be blessed with strong, virtuous and heroic children." Meredith.

"Let us take the sixth step for self-restraint and longevity." Mark.

"Finally, let us take the seventh step and be true companions and remain lifelong partners by this wedlock." Meredith.

"We have taken the Seven Steps. You have become mine forever." Meredith and Mark faced each other as they recited together. They handed the eagle feathers back to the elder who exchanged it for a small engraved tablet. Turning again to one another they read the Ojibwe prayer. Meredith began:

"Oh Great Spirit, whose voice I hear in the winds, and whose breath gives life to everyone, hear me. I come to you as one of your many children. I am weak. I am small. I need your wisdom and your strength. Let me walk in beauty, and make my eyes ever behold the red and purple sunsets. Make my hands respect the things you have made, and make my ears sharp so that I may hear your voice."

Mark took the tablet and continued: "Make me wise so that I may understand what you have taught my people and the lessons you have hidden in each leaf and rock. I ask for wisdom and strength, not to be superior to my brothers, but to be able to fight my greatest enemy, myself. Make me ever ready to come before you with clean hands and a straight eye, so as life fades away as a fading sunset, my spirit may come to you without shame."

During Mark's reading, Meredith could not withhold her tears. Nor could Karen. She approached the bride, took the tablet, and quickly wiped her daughter's cheeks and returned to her seat. The couple stood holding hands for the blessing.

"Please rise for the final blessing from the tribe and from the church." Tom reached out and placed a hand on the shoulder of the bride and groom:

"Now you will feel no rain, for each of you will be shelter for the other.

Now you will feel no cold, for each of you will be warmth to the other.

Now there will be no loneliness, for each of you will be companion to the other.

Now you are two persons, but there is only one life before you.

May beauty surround you both in the journey ahead and through all the years.

May happiness be your companion and your days be long upon the earth.

Elders, please bring the blankets."

Nakomis and Bobby came forward each carrying a small blue blanket which they draped over first Meredith's then Mark's shoulders. The elders then escorted the couple to the fire pit where gentle flames had been dancing throughout the ceremony. Bride and groom slid the single blue blankets from shoulder to fire. Nakomis and Bobby spread a soft white double blanket over the couple. Grandmother spoke the words of the Native American blessing symbolized by the blanket: "Each of you will be warmth to the other." Wrapped together in the white blanket, the married couple walked as one back to the arbor. The minister raised a hand of blessing over their heads:

"May the Lord bless you and keep you. May the Lord make his face to shine upon you and be gracious to you. May the Lord lift up his countenance upon you and give you peace. Amen." A number of attendees repeated the "Amen."

To Mark: "You may kiss the bride." And he did. In fact, this was the most rehearsed part of the ceremony. Flute and drum music signaling the recessional was in competition with the native shouts of joy from the groom's side of the gathering and the enthusiastic applause from the bride's.

The staff of Green Gardens ushered the crowd into the clear-roofed open-air tent next to the farmhouse where they nibbled on hors-d'oeuvres of wild mushrooms, onions, and goat cheeses while the wedding party posed for photos in addition to those taken during the ceremony. Afterward, a hybrid wedding feast awaited the wedding party and their guests. There were a few toasts made to the couple. Then while the guests indulged in venison with juniper berries, fry bread, squash casserole, Three Sisters Soup of corn, beans, celery, onion, pumpkin and sage, fresh berries and wild rice pudding among other delicacies and succulent dishes, Meredith and Mark, with help from Jenny, distributed gifts. Each guest received a small porcupine quill basket with a floral or animal design woven into the lid.

The festivities lasted into the night, with native chanting and dancing. But for Meredith the highlight of the evening was her mother's performance at a little spinet piano of popular American love songs. As the fervor begin to wind down, instead of leaving for a honeymoon, Meredith and Mark retreated to Karen and Bobby's house exhausted. Mark explained that it was traditional for the couple to spend time with the bride's family after the wedding.

"This suits me just fine." Meredith with her long fringe plopped onto the couch.

"You'll have a ton of wedding gifts to open tomorrow," Karen said, "but there's one Bobby and I want you guys to have tonight." She exchanged glances with her husband.

"Well, bring it on with some scissors for ribbon-cutting." Meredith hadn't the energy to protest.

"You won't need scissors. It's not wrapped." Karen reached out for Bobby to take her hand. "You see, as a wedding present,

Bobby and I are giving you and Mark . . .Baldwin Lake Lodge.

* * *

As wedding images dissipated, Meredith awoke realizing she had responsibilities now. Managing the lodge had been easy and fun up until now. The bear mauling had changed that. The gravity of her situation took full possession of her thinking. In the shower, she kept asking herself over and over, *Why did the bear attack Billy? Unprovoked bear attacks are unheard of. Something attracted him to Billy and not the others. Why did Terrence disappear? Why was Terrence so eager to get to Wheeler Lake? Jake didn't think he was chased by the bear, so where did he go? And what became of him?*

As she slid into her jeans and pulled on a flannel shirt, she promised herself to find answers and solve these mysteries. Then she went to eat a hearty wilderness breakfast.

Chapter Four
Eric's Journey

"We've been over and over this, Eric. You have to do it. The cops are convinced that you're the perp."

"And you know I'm innocent."

"Of course I know you didn't kill Sandy. I believe you. You're my brother and I'm telling you, they are going to arrest you. They're not looking for the real killer any more. They have plenty of evidence to convict you. You've got to go in hiding while the P.I. finds the one who did it. This guy is good, Eric. He'll find him and you'll be exonerated."

"Won't leaving the country make me look even more guilty? They have the knife with my prints on it and my wife's blood on my clothes. Plus I have no alibi. And then there's the insurance policy. That gives them motive. For the police, judge and jury it's a slam dunk."

"Look. When my guy finds who did this, you can come back from Canada a free man. Just take these." He pushed a small brown package toward his brother. "I went to a lot of trouble and dealt with some questionable characters to get you a fake passport and driver's license—by the way your name is Terrence McElvin—and got you in with a couple of guys going fishing at a outpost in Manitoba not far from a hunting cabin. You'll meet up with them at the airport tomorrow and fly with them out of Chicago to Winnipeg. So call your top mechanic and put him in charge of the collision shop—now! I've put rods, reels, a loaded tackle box, and a duffle bag full of fishing clothes in my car.

"Wait a minute, Alan, my attorney will convince them I am not a flight risk. I am a business owner, respected in the community, I have no priors, so they'll let me out on bond. If I skip town, even if they find the killer, I'll go to jail."

"Better some community service, or at best a year or two in jail, than lethal injection or life! For God's sake, man, just do it!! All documents, plane ticket, and information about the fishing trip and what to do afterwards are in this packet. Study it tonight and I'll pick you up in the morning and take you to the airport. Be ready at nine o'clock sharp. Remember. The minute we reach the airport, you're Terrence, not Eric. Not until you get back home. Now this is crucial: *don't tell anyone anything about your real life*. Not even the tiniest little detail. It could cost you everything. And don't worry about your kid. Kathy and I will take good care of her. Rebecca thinks her mother is visiting relatives in Maine. Best that you should be the one to tell her the truth when the time comes."

"I can't believe you're doing all this for me."

"You're the big brother who took care of me when I was a teenage troublemaker. You were always the good one—and you still are. We're going to prove that."

* * *

What am I doing? That bear is about to eat Billy and I'm running the other way to save my own skin. I am double fugitive. But it's too late now. I have to do this.

Eric reached the edge of Wheeler Lake. He set down his rods and tackle box. The path continued to the right along the shore. He abandoned the fishing gear and followed the eastern shore as instructed in the information packet provided by his brother. His footsteps crunched in the soft underbrush. A gaggle of Canada geese flew up honking their alarm at his intrusion.

"Shut up, you guys. You'll signal the bear where I am!"

He reached a flat area where the geese had been resting and depositing their droppings. Easy going but messy. Then some dense shrubbery made it almost impossible to stick close to the lake like the directions said to do. Eric pushed his way through some large fern-like plants and got back to the lakeshore. The rocky lakeshore. Hunched over, using his hands and feet he scrabbled over the rocky outcroppings. When he was able to stand up again, there it was. The logging road that would lead the three miles into Ontario and on to the hunting cabin. Eric closed his eyes and let out a long breath of relief. A little glow of hope spread in his chest. But it was short-lived.

Here I am alone in the middle of the wilderness not far from a vicious bear and who-knows-what other dangerous creatures. I have no idea where I am. I've got to walk another four or five miles to some cabin owned by a guy I don't even know. I don't even know for sure the cabin exists or, if it does, if I'll be able to find it. And then . . . . I can't waste my time thinking. I've got to move.

The logging road was nothing more than two parallel ruts for the logging truck tires. Weeds and grasses had grown high in between. Except for an occasional mud puddle, the ruts offered an easy path. Eric found it helpful to jog in one of the ruts rather than walk. He made up a little tune and sang to keep himself company:

"Jogging on the logging, jogging on the logging. I'm jogging on the logging road.

Make it to the cabin, make it to the cabin, I'll make it to the cabin soon."

That didn't last long. His breath became too valuable a commodity. A little hill loomed ahead. Eric shortened his stride for the incline. Cresting the top of the hill he stopped dead still. The ugliest creature he had ever seen stood in the middle of the road staring at him. It had the appearance of a lumpy horse with a fat face. But it was big and didn't look friendly. Eric dared not move or make a sound. Neither did equus. In the physical paralysis of fear Eric's mind raced to identify the animal. A moose. A female moose.

A movement by the side of the road. Out of the corner of his eye he saw a smaller version of the thing standing in front of him.

Her calf. I'm in trouble now.

The moose cow pawed the ground with one hoof. Instinctively Eric sat down and began to eat some of the grass from between the ruts hoping to show he was no threat to her or her young.

After an eternity and a throat full of dry weeds, Eric watched the cow move toward her calf. The two disappeared into the bush.

Eric waited to be sure she was gone before collapsing on his side. He became aware of how fast and hard his heart was beating. *Need to rest a minute. Get my wind back.* From where he lay he could see the trees from bottom to top. Perched on a huge clump of sticks, moss, grass and mud in a poplar tree, a large bird with a white head was eyeing him. *Bald eagle I bet. And its sitting on a large nest. Powerful-looking bird.* "Don't worry. I won't hurt you or your babies. I won't hurt anything or anybody. I didn't kill my wife. I loved her. I loved her." Eric found himself talking out loud to the eagle who swooped off the nest with a high-pitched squeal and soared up above Eric. He watched it circle, wishing he could fly too. Fly on to the cabin, or back home, or back in time.

On his feet again he realized he was hungry. He took off his backpack and found a package of peanut butter crackers and a small can of apple juice. "This will help me get there." He wondered if he had crossed into Ontario. Not that he expected to find a province line marker in the wilderness saying "Welcome to Ontario," but he must be getting close. A short distance ahead he came to another lake. Not as big as Cinnamon, but big enough to house a resident loon. Eric stopped to admire the black and white band around its neck and the way it could dive under so silently and stay under so long. It surprised him by coming up practically in front of him. It then stood up on the water and flapped its wings wildly, cawing like a madman.

"You are quite a water dancer, my friend." The loon went under again and Eric resumed his journey. Somehow watching the loon had lightened the heaviness in his heart and soul. "Thank you, God, for your beautiful creatures. I guess even the moose cow is beautiful in her own way. At least to a bull moose anyway." Then he thought of the bear and was piqued again by remorse for not trying to help Billy. "Please, God, let Billy be okay." Eric wasn't a praying man. He went to mass with Sandy only on rare occasions. Being alone in the pristine wilderness had given him clarity of mind and vision. Here could sense the Divine plan. He determined that if he got clear of this crime, he would make some changes in his life. Right now he needed to find that cabin and get out of danger.

The epiphany brought on by his encounter with the loon soon dissipated. The farther he went, the more afraid and insecure he felt. *What if Alan's directions are incorrect? What if his friend told him wrong? I'll die here and never be found!* Despite his fears Eric pushed on. Just as despair was taking hold, he spotted a little wooden gate that opened onto a worn pathway. He rushed to the gate. The cabin was set back about fifty feet from the logging road, just like the directions said. The windows of the whole-log cabin were boarded up but the front door was not.

In his backpack Eric found a small envelope containing two keys. One fit the dead bolt on the front door. He wasn't sure what the other unlocked.

The one big room inside was sparsely furnished. An iron cot with mattress rolled up at the foot, a couple of wooden chairs and table, a shelf with a butane burner, two china plates and some mismatched flatware. The one redeeming feature was a huge stone fireplace. There were some half-burned candles on the table. Matches on the shelf. Eric lit a couple of candles, sat on one of the chairs, and closed his eyes. *The rest of the trip will not be so hard. I flew to Winnipeg, met Billy and Jake, flew into Baldwin Lake with all the lodge guests who had come for a pricey week. A pretty young lady pilot got us to Cinnamon in a float plane. The week with the guys went okay. I escaped a bear attack, had a showdown with a moose, hiked four or five miles and found the cabin. Can't believe I've done all that. But I'm safe now. Really tired and need some sleep.* Eric put his head back against the wall and slept.

Sandy was with him on the logging road. They were laughing about eating grass to fool the moose. Then blood appeared on Sandy's clothes. And on his. Suddenly the eagle swooped down, grabbed Sandy in its talons, flew up with a high-pitched squeal and was gone. Eric was left alone on the logging road in the middle of the Canadian wilderness holding a bloody knife. He awoke with a jolt. His face, neck, and top of his sweatshirt were soaked in tears. . . . tears of grief he could no longer hold in. He put his head between his hands and sobbed—deep, painful sobs.

* * *

Behind the cabin he discovered the shed mentioned in the instructions. The second key opened the padlock. Eric let out a long whistle of amazement. A shiny red UTV was waiting to take him on the next leg of the journey.

"Wow. A Massimo T-Boss 550. Roof and all. Alan's friend ain't cheap!" Eric inspected the vehicle with a mechanic's eye. "This baby has hardly been used. Keys in the ignition, ready to go. And she'll go. About forty-five mph." Next to the UTV stood a not-so-new snowmobile. "Won't need that." He found several full gas containers in the shed, loaded them in the back of the UTV, and returned to the cabin to retrieve his backpack. He ate the last pack of crackers and drank the last can of apple juice. "Okay. Let's continue with this insane adventure."

He started up the UTV, pulled it just outside the shed, closed the door and snapped the padlock shut. He hated to leave the security of the cabin, but according to the plan, he needed to be in Kenora by nightfall. That would be around ten p.m. He looked at his watch. Five hours. He hoped that would be enough time to reach his destination and that there would be no delays or disasters. A hand-drawn map of the route was in his hoodie pocket. Eric took it out and unfolded it. He was to continue east on the logging road until it ended at a wider and flatter north-south dirt road. He would not come to a town for about three hours., according to a note scrawled on the map. "Hope they have something to eat there and take credit cards."

Eric found himself smiling as he turned the vehicle onto the rutted logging road. Blessed hope had returned. The late afternoon sun coming low through the tall boreal trees cast a golden glow and warmed his spirit. He was lucky with the weather so far. But he was prepared for rain. Alan had packed a plastic parka that fit into an envelope-sized pouch. There was plenty of gas. Nothing to worry about right now. He had survived. He had found the cabin. He was no longer hiking. He had wheels.

He was cruising about thirty miles per hour when he hit the hydraulic brakes hard almost dumping himself out. An adult brown duck with a dark stripe above her eye and mottled feather markings had ventured onto the logging road with a string of five ducklings in a straight line behind her. Walking without a care in the world, unconcerned with the idling UTV, they let out intermittent little quacks and took their own sweet time reaching the other side where they fanned out and began pecking and picking up morsels of something in the grasses.

"You guys are something else! Just look at you. Not a care in the world. Momma, aren't you worried about that eagle scooping up one of your babies? If you are, you certainly don't show it. I should be more like you. If I hadn't been so worried about getting the cars repaired on time, I would have been home the night Sandy . . . ." Eric stopped the one-sided conversation with the ducks. "Can't think about that now. Got to concentrate on getting to Kenora." He eased on the gas and drove slowly past Momma and her kids only to stop again about twenty yards farther. An adult duck of the same species was sitting in the middle of the road. It tried to run from the noisy vehicle but could not. Eric got off the UTV and slowly approached the duck. Again it tried to flee but gave up. Eric could see that that one leg was broken and a wing was slack, too. "I can fix any car and get it going again, but I know nothing about repairing ducks. But hold on, little fellow." He found a small roll of duct tape in the storage compartment of the UTV. Alan had thought to pack a Swiss army knife and Eric had thought to put it in his backpack. He cut a strip of tape and managed to hold the animal still enough to wind it around the injured leg. "This duct tape—or *duck* tape—might work. But sorry I can't do anything about the wing." He backed up to allow the bird one more attempt to get away. It was able to hobble to the roadside, through the bushes and into some shallow water which spread out into a small lake. Eric spotted the female and her line of ducklings in the deeper water. "Go, Daddy. Go join your family. Wish I could join mine."

Not long after the duck and duckling incidents, the road passed by a larger lake. Eric slowed looking for another loon. Instead he found a brown furry head sailing along in the calm water with a leafy branch in its mouth. Eric hopped out of the vehicle to get a closer look, but the head went under and a large, round, flat tail came up, slapped the water hard and disappeared.

"I know what you are, Mr. Beaver! I bet you're building a lodge or maybe a dam. In a couple of minutes the head came back swimming in the opposite direction, went under, came back up with another branch and started back in the original direction. Eric moved closer to the edge of the lake and watched for the beaver. Now he could see the structure being built. A mound of large and small branches a short distance up the shoreline.

"I bet that's your new home, buddy! Good job!" Eric watched the beaver's back-and-forth swims for a few more minutes then resumed his road trip. He found himself smiling again. Watching these forest animals lifted his heart.

Just as he got back on the road, he noticed the wind rising and the sun fading. Within a minute, raindrops hit his face. He stopped to reach in the backpack. Before he could grab the poncho pack and open it, the rain came sudden, thick, and fast. He could not see the road before him. Even though he managed to get the poncho out and on, it was too little too late. He was soaked. The vehicle inched forward. The ruts were filling with rainwater making it difficult to position the four-wheeler correctly in the ruts. One major misjudgment and the UTV would fall over, dumping driver and cargo into the mud. The rain felt cold and the absence of sun caused the temperature to drop. Eric's hoodie and poncho afforded little warmth. His teeth began to chatter from the cold but also from nerves. This was scary. The rain was so thick that he could not discern the edge of the roadway. He had to stop. The roof offered no protection from the blowing rain. He folded his hands over the top of the steering wheel and put his forehead against them. Nothing to do but wait it out. He sat listening to rumbles of thunder and the rain pounding the roof of the UTV.

Almost as abruptly as it started the squall ended. He lifted his head and glanced up at the little piece of sky he could see between the tall trees of the boreal forest. A few wispy black clouds were disintegrating before a renewed blue sky. "Okay. I see now what they mean by unpredictable Canadian weather." Eric took off the wet poncho and found his hoodie to be equally wet. He couldn't get the poncho back in the pouch but managed to get it in the backpack. He set out again.

It was only a short distance from there to the end of the logging road. After checking the now-soggy penciled map, Eric turned south on a flat dirt and gravel road. Much smoother going. A provincial route that would eventually become paved and dovetail into Canada Highway 17 to Kenora. "Praise to you, Lord Jesus Christ." A response from the Mass came to his lips. He was ecstatic to see electric poles and lines along the roadside. Simple little houses grew closer together. A First-Nations village. It wasn't much of a commercial town, but there was a gas station with a Coca-Cola sign. Eric pulled up, cut the motor and went in.

A guy with thick arms hung over the counter reading a newspaper. A young aboriginal woman was counting money from an old-fashioned cash register.

"Excuse me. Do you take credit cards?" The man looked up and took a minute to scrutinize this customer from out of nowhere.

"Not American Express. Visa's okay."

Eric purchased bread, peanut butter and jelly, an ice cream sandwich and a Coke. His Visa worked fine. "How far to Kenora?" The store clerk looked out at the UTV. "About an hour and a half in that thing."

He was right. At 9:30 p.m. it was still faint daylight when Eric hit Highway 17 heading into Kewatin, Kenora's next-door-neighbor city. There were slight cliffs on each side where the road cut through. Eric was startled when a creature came down a low embankment and walked—not ran—across the roadway. Eric slowed. A wolf. An old wolf. Bare patches in its fur, a slight limp, ribs visible. A scrawny, sad-looking wolf. It didn't seem to care about people or vehicles or anything.

"Exiled from your pack? Too old? Can't hunt anymore, huh? Going off to die?" The wolf walked along the side of the road until it came to a spot where it could disappear into the woods. "Don't give up, old fellow. Don't ever give up." *And neither will I.*

Ten minutes later Eric, now Terrence, pulled up in front of a large two-story yellow and white house on a small lot just off the main street in Kenora. A pretty white sign with painted blue flowers out front read "Margie's Rooms and Meals." Eric double checked the address on his map, grabbed his backpack and rang the doorbell. It made the traditional Big Ben ding-dong tones.

A pleasant-looking woman in her early to mid-forties or so opened the door. Brown hair, hazel eyes, no make-up. Warm smile.

"You must be Terrence McElvin. I'm Margaret Taylor. Please come in. Your room is ready."

Eric stepped into the hallway.

"Have you had a long journey?"

"Yes, Ma'am, I have."

"Well, go on up. It's the first one on the right. The door is open. Relax a bit, change clothes if you like while I heat you up some dinner."

"Thank you, but I have stuff for a peanut butter and jelly sandwich."

"Nonsense. I have some hearty beef stew, homemade dinner rolls, and fresh blueberry pie. You could use a hot meal. If you'll give me the key to your vehicle I'll take it around back and lock it in the garage. You won't have to worry about it. I'll tap at your door when dinner's ready."

"You're very kind, Mrs. . . . ." Eric couldn't remember her last name.

"Just call me Margie."

Eric handed her the key to the UTV.

Chapter Five
Hospital Visit

"We found his rods and tackle box down by Wheeler Lake." The SAR chief of operations sat the missing man's fishing gear down on the back stoop of the lodge. "But no other sign of him. Guess he left these so he could run from the bear. Musta realized that staying alive is more important than catching a fish, right? Oh, and just so you know, I'm pulling my people out before sundown. Can't keep 'em in the bush more than twelve hours. Tomorrow we'll bring in the chopper." He headed back to the floatplane dock before Meredith could respond. She brought the rods and tackle box inside and opened the box. Right on top she found a Manitoba fishing license. *Name: Terrence McElvin.* Jake had told them the other man's name was Terrence. So those were the names of the three guys: Billy, the victim, Jake, the one in the tree, and Terrence, the missing one. She would never forget those names.

Terrence, I want so much to be out there looking for you, but the business of the lodge goes on. With today being change-over day, I've got guests departing and guests arriving. So many details to manage I can't take time out. Please let them find you. The lodge can't afford to have guests disappearing. And a bear attack is really bad for the guy but also bad for our business.

Meredith closed the box. A buzzing noise increasing in volume told her that the wheeled commercial plane carrying this week's guests was coming in. She needed to be at the deplaning/boarding zone. She hurried into the office, grabbed the list of new guests and rushed to greet them. Even as the new arrivals were deplaning, her head was full of questions. *What made that bear attack? There have been several instances of bears coming around the outpost cabins looking for food. But never an attack. On a human who had no food with him? And why Billy and not one of the others? I've got to get answers to these questions.*

The arriving guests had questions of their own:

"Have you found the guy?" "Did you find the bear?" "Did you shoot the bear?" "How many people did the bear actually attack?" And the one that hit Meredith the hardest:

"Have you had many cancellations since the bear attack?" She tried to give gracious but non-committal answers. Meredith didn't expect them to know anything about it. *News sure travels fast. It just happened yesterday.*

One by one the guides gathered the luggage and escorted the new guests to their cabins. The departing guests were more considerate of her situation and didn't bombard her with questions. Instead they thanked her for a wonderful week and wished her well. Maybe they were just tired from a week of long days fishing. So many of the guests were returnees year after year and had become like old friends. Some had been coming since she was a child. A few even brought little gifts—books for the lodge bookshelf, framed pictures of trophies they caught, homemade candies, exotic pantry items, an occasional bottle of spirits. They appreciated the fine service they had received from Karen and Bobby over the years. Meredith hoped that she and Mark would live up to the reputation.

Back at the lodge she found Karen in the lounge area chatting with a couple of arriving guests who didn't seem in any particular hurry to get out there fishing.

"Mama, can I ask a favor?"

"Sure, Sweetie."

"Will you and Bobby run things here until tomorrow? I really think Mark and I should go to the hospital in Winnipeg to check on Billy. Get more details on what happened and why. He might even have an idea where Terrence is."

"No problem. If you want to fly out with the plane that just came in, you'd better go on and pack an overnight bag for you and Mark. Everything will be fine here." She gave her daughter one of those mothering smiles. "I think Bobby and I can handle it."

"Thanks, Mama. You're always my angel from heaven!"

Mark was only too happy to comply with Meredith's spur-of-the-moment decision. They found the pilot in the kitchen finishing up a snack and explained things to him. No objection on his part. There were extra seats for the return trip to Winnipeg.

In a few minutes they were skyward. Meredith took a little note pad and pencil out of her carry-on.

"Let's make a list of the questions to ask Billy."

"If he's able to talk and if the doctors will allow it."

"That reminds me. We need to make a list of what to ask the doctor, too."

By the time the both lists were complete, they were at the Winnipeg airport.

* * *

"He's lost a lot of blood, he has a punctured lung, and sustained severe lacerations on his back and hands. He must have used his hands to cover the back of his head and neck. Probably saved his life. The right shoulder was dislocated and the muscles and tendons partially torn away. We did surgery on that. Between the shoulder and the back, he's had a lot of sutures. It's too early to tell about the extent of the injuries to the back, but I think the spinal cord is intact." The doctor, still in his blood-stained surgical clothes and mask down around his neck, was very forthcoming about Billy's prognosis: "Right now he's in stable condition, but we're watching him. He did receive a blood transfusion and he needs oxygen and a respirator, but I'm convinced he'll make a full recovery. He'll live with a lot of scar tissue."

"Is he able to talk to us, doctor? As owners of the lodge and outpost we need to find out exactly what happened and why," Mark explained.

"I'll have the nurse remove the respirator for a few minutes. He has just come out of surgery and needs rest. Go easy."

"Of course, doctor. We just have a few quick questions." Meredith held the note paper with the lists in her hand.

"The nurse will take you to him." The doctor started to walk away then turned back around to them.

"One thing I might mention. The patient smelled terrible. He had evidently rubbed some kind of liquid on his arms, hands, and face. It may have been insect repellent. I've sent it to the lab, but maybe he could tell you. I know you must be concerned for your guest but also for your business. I'm very sorry."

He disappeared through swinging double doors.

"Well, we didn't need a list of questions for him. He answered everything and then some before we asked."

A nurse in scrubs beckoned to them. They followed her into a small private room. Billy lay reclined at a forty-five-degree angle, eyes closed, oxygen tube in his nose, respirator over his mouth, an IV running from the back of one hand. The nurse removed the respirator, punched a few buttons on the bedside machine, and exited.

"I'll be back in five minutes." She left the room door open.

Meredith and Mark approached the patient, one on each side of the bed.

"Billy? Can you talk to us for a minute?"

"It's Mark and Meredith, owners of Baldwin Lake Lodge," Meredith added to Mark's question.

Billy opened his eyes half way. They were pretty bloodshot. "Yeah, okay." Closed again.

"I am so terribly sorry this happened to you. I would give anything to undo it. In the twenty-five-plus years my family has owned and operated the lodge and outposts, there has never been a bear attack. We're hoping you can help us understand why this happened." Meredith glanced at Mark then at her list.

"Bear didn't like me," Billy mumbled.

"Do you know why he didn't like you? Why did he go for you and neither of the other two?"

"Musta been that stuff."

"What stuff, Billy?' Mark took a step closer to hear the answer.

"That stuff in the bottle in the kitchen cabinet. What happened to the other guys?" His eyes opened again, wider.

"Jake climbed a tree, and Terrence . . . well, Terrence ran away."

"So they're okay?"

"Perfectly. But we need to ask you if you have any idea where Terrence could have gone. He's still missing."

"Something wasn't right with him. Didn't seem to enjoy fishing. Too anxious to get to the other lake. Kinda kept to himself. Just a little off." Billy swallowed hard. Talking had made his throat dry. He seemed to have trouble breathing.

"Honey, we should call the nurse," Mark said.

"You're right, Mark. Will you go find her?" Meredith reached out and put her hand on top of Billy's—the one without the IV.

"Doctor says you're going to be fine. Just rest and recuperate. Thank you for talking with us."

"No, thank *you*, Miss, for saving me."

Meredith patted his hand. The nurse came in and hurried to replace the respirator.

As they passed the nurses' station on the way out, the surgeon called to them.

"Excuse me. Do you have moose hunting at your lodge?"

"Yes. In the season. If there's a demand for it." Mark answered.

"The lab identified that substance on the patient's body as moose estrous. Just thought you'd want to know."

"Moose tags start in September. Billy had come to fish."

"Strange, huh?" The doctor smiled, turned on his heel, and left the couple to ponder the puzzle.

* * *

Both Meredith and Mark were of few words over coffee in the hospital cafeteria. They sat, stirring and staring into the cup. Meredith was the first to break the silence.

"Well, we came to get answers, and all we got was more questions. Moose estrous? Why and how, for Pete's sake."

Mark looked up at her. "I've been thinking. Some hunters bring it with them when going for moose. They put it on themselves or on something thinking it will attract a big bull moose. Hunters have used the cabin at Cinnamon. Maybe they left some behind . . ."

"And Billy rubbed it on supposing it to be bug spray."

"Right. And doc did say he thought at first it might be insect repellent."

"Good thinking, Mark. Would that be the reason the bear went for him and not the others?"

"Most likely. Bear was probably hoping for a moose calf dinner."

A petite thirty-something-looking woman with a blond pixie cut came over to their table.

"Hi. Are you the owners of Baldwin Lake Lodge?"

"We are."

"I'm Sarah, Billy's wife. I flew up as soon as they notified me." She stuck out a hand first to Mark then to Meredith.

"First of all, thank you for rescuing my husband. I'm sure he would have died if you hadn't gone to check on the men." She looked from Meredith to Mark. "And thank you both for coming to see him here in the hospital."

"We are so very sorry, Sarah. We will do anything to make this better for you. We are refunding the entire amount of Billy's trip, his and the other two men," Mark said.

"Oh, how are they doing?"

"One is fine, absolutely no harm done. We haven't located the third party yet, but . . . uh . . . we're sure he's okay, too." Meredith sent Mark a help-me-out-here look.

"We're also upgrading his—and your flight home to first class," he added.

"That's absolutely not necessary. Anyway, thank you again for all you've done. I'd better get back to Billy." Her smile could not hide the worry. She headed for the elevators.

"I know what you're thinking. But I took care of the refunds and the airline business on line this morning at the lodge."

"My darling husband, you amaze me. Let's go get a decent meal somewhere. I'm starving."

"I second that."

The meal at Rae and Jerry's Steak House did not distract them from the bear incident.

"This whole thing is getting more and more bizarre. Moose estrous. And now Terrence 'a little off.' I wasn't able to notify his family because we don't have any contact information from him or Jake. Billy was in charge of the party of three." Meredith had hardly touched her filet in spite of her professed starvation.

"We should have asked Billy for Terrence's contact information, but he was in no condition to remember details like that."

"You know, Mark, they're calling off the ground search at sundown today. Gonna use copters for a couple of days. I arranged for us to fly back with them tomorrow morning. We have to be at the heliport before six a.m. We'd better go to our hotel and get some sleep."

"You reserved the hotel, too?"

"I did."

"My darling wife, you amaze me."

* * *

Kenora

The room was large with a triple window decorated with white organdy curtains and old-fashioned pull-down shades. Eric was surprised to find a four-poster double bed with a sparkling white chenille bedspread that added to the brightness of the room. A neatly folded gray and white blanket lay draped across the foot of the bed. There were matching bedside tables with matching lamps, a wooden rocking chair with a blue and gray throw. An overstuffed armchair faced a small television on a stand. A rectangular table in the corner next to the bathroom door held a hotplate and teapot. In the opposite corner stood a sturdy wooden chest-of-drawers. A hairbrush lay on top of the chest. The polished hardwood floor was almost completely covered by a colorful oriental rug. Although the house was old, Eric noticed a nice fresh smell to the room.

In the backpack he had put a clean T-shirt, but no other clothing to change into. He took off the still-damp hoodie and shirt and switched to the clean one. He used the restroom and brushed his hair. No sooner had he sprawled out on the bed, than he heard a tapping at the door.

"Mr. McElvin, dinner's ready." Margie's voice was soft and musical.

"Be right down."

After the food in the outpost and the crackers and juice on the road, Margie's dinner seemed like the best meal he had ever eaten.

"The beef in this stew is fantastic. So tender and juicy and full of flavor."

"That's Alberta beef. It's high-quality grass-fed. Only kind I buy. Glad you like it."

"And your dinner rolls. Did you bake them?"

"I did. I love to make all kinds of bread. Love the smell of rising dough. Can I get you a second helping of stew?"

"No, Ma'am. Your first helping was more than generous."

She sat the blueberry pie in front of him.

"Now this I didn't make. I ordered it from the Second Street Bakery. You'll want to try it for breakfast or lunch. Wonderful breads, pastries, and desserts. Good coffee, too."

Eric took a bite. "This is delicious. The blueberry flavor is intense."

"Wild Canadian blueberries. They're in season now. Bears love them."

Eric choked a little at that remark, nevertheless he ate and savored the pie.

"I thought I was a pretty good cook, but you put me to shame, Margie. Now how do I pay you for this?"

"The money order I received covered lodging and dinner for a month. So you owe me nothing for four weeks. Just let me know if you have any food allergies, likes or dislikes."

"I think I would like anything you cook. May I help you with the clean-up and dishes?"

"Nonsense. You are tired and sleepy. Go on to your room and get a good night's sleep. There will be coffee on the stove and muffins on the table starting at seven. That's included."

"Then goodnight. See you in the morning."

Eric lay on the clean-smelling bed in his boxers and the one clean T-shirt. His mind wouldn't shut down. He was overwhelmed to find himself in the midst of such civility. Fine food and accommodations. What a contrast to the past week. He was surprised at the empathy he felt for the creatures of the boreal forest and their struggles, identifying his own with theirs. He somehow felt connected to it all.

"I guess it's the call of the wild," he told himself. At the outpost he was absorbed in his own innocence and guilt— innocent of the murder, guilty of the illegal flight. On the journey to Kenora the basic survival instinct removed him from all other concerns. He thought of the moose, the ducks, the loon, the beaver, and even the bedraggled wolf. How each made his spirit rise. He felt lucky—even blessed—to have experienced the journey. It would live within him forever. He would share it with Becca. He would bring his daughter to the wilderness one day.

Unable to sleep, he clicked on the bedside light and cut on the TV. A newscaster was reporting local accidents, fires, lost dogs and the like. Eric's eyes began to close.

Elsewhere in eastern Manitoba the victim of a bear attack at Cinnamon Lake was rescued by the Baldwin Lake lodge owner. He was rushed to the hospital in Winnipeg where sources say he is in critical condition. One of his fishing partners managed to escape unharmed. A third partner is still missing. More on this as the story develops.

Eric was wide awake now, sweating, heart pounding.

"My God! I forgot all about Billy! Here I am enjoying good food and modern comforts while Billy is in a hospital in critical condition fighting for his life!" He pictured a hospital room, Billy lying in a bed with all sorts of tubes connected to him, machines beeping, family members crying.

"I left him. I didn't even try to help him. But what could I have done? I ran from the murder of my wife, I ran from the bear mauling Billy. What kind of person am I?"

Eric slid to his knees beside the bed. "Oh, God, forgive me for being so selfish. Please let Billy get well. Don't let his injuries be too serious. And if you can, tell Sandy that I'm sorry I spent so much time at the shop and neglected her and Rebecca. I'm sorry, I'm so sorry . . . ."

The tears came. Tears of grief, remorse, and exhaustion.

Chapter Six
Kuru

Kuru was really hungry. He was always hungry, except during the long white-season sleep. He had passed through a successful coupling period, enjoyed warm naps in the sun, and lived off of roots, bugs, worms, and a few scurrying creatures with tails—some with fur-covered tails, some without. Then the luscious berries. So delicious. He had eaten, and eaten, and eaten them. But now he wanted something more substantial. He wanted meat. Fresh, young, tender meat. He envisioned a small flattail[1]. "Flattail meat is tasty, but those flattails are a lot of work. I have to tear up the log nest, get in the water, and hunt for the babies. The big ones have teeth that can give a bad bite." He thought for a minute. "A tova[2]. That's the best meat. That's what I want."

Lowering his head, he used his muzzle to turn over a mossy log. The little white larvae squirmed around trying to go deeper into the ground. Kuru licked up a mouthful. With a paw he turned over another log. Another mouthful of larvae. This was not satisfying.

Kuru was disappointed and frustrated. He was not overly concerned with the taste of food, only the amount in his mouth and stomach mattered. It signaled most of his behavior. He wanted quantity not quality, volume not flavor. Worms and insects made little difference in his foodometer.

"I won't be ready for the long white sleep. I have to find me a flattail or a tova."

So he determined to spend the day looking for one or the other. His nose was the guiding light to food-finding. He could

---

[1] flattail = beaver. See *Poplar River* Chapter 4.
[2] tova = moose calf. See *Poplar River* Chapter 6

detect a long-eared hopper[3] or a bush-tailed tree climber[4] on the other side of the lake if the wind were blowing this way. He often sensed tempting aromas from the big, square uprights' nest[5], but he feared the firesticks[6]. Uprights use them to take the life force out of kodas[7] and and long claws[8]. He had heard stories of his forbearers that fell victim to the uprights' firesticks. So he stayed clear of the uprights' nest. That would be a last resort.

Kuru went to his favorite fishing spot—a flat rock beside a stream that rippled into the lake. Maybe he would be lucky enough to find a shiny swimmer[9] or two. That would hold him until he could get himself some meat. He put his front paws into the rippling water and went on the alert for wiggling objects. He swatted at one and missed, but he kept his vision trained on the water. Another. Missed. After what seemed like a long wait, a large black swimmer[10] heading upstream was slowed by the current. Putting his curved claws together Kuru formed a trap, leaving just enough room for the swimmer to enter. When it did, the claws clamped together. Kuru stuck his snout into the water, took the swimmer in his jaws, and pulled the wiggler into shallow water where he could easily devour it.

Prompted by this success, he continued fishing until he had eaten two more swimmers. Now he was tired of the work and bored by the fare the rapids offered. He felt a little sleepy and opted for a nap. He found a jackpine that had dropped enough needles to form a cushioned bed and lay down on his belly. A soft breeze caressed his face and sent him into an indolent state that soon became a vision world.

He was shuffling along the lakeside following the scent of a young tova. He spotted the youngster drinking his fill of lake

---

[3] long-eared hopper = rabbit
[4] bush-tailed tree climber = squirrel
[5] upright = human, nest = cabin
[6] firesticks = rifles
[7] koda = bull moose
[8] long claw = bear
[9] shiny swimmer = fish (walleye)
[10] black swimmer = fish (northern pike)

water. Kuru kept his distance, circling around to be in position to spring on his victim from behind. He watched, waiting for his instincts to give the go signal. Saliva was rushing into his mouth. His eyes widened and his lips pulled back. He sprang. His claws pulled him up on the tova's back and his fangs went into the neck. But the tova turned. It was not a tova. It was an upright and it had a firestick!

Kuru jerked himself out of sleep. He was in a panic, blowing, muscles contracting. He looked around. No upright. No firestick. He realized then it was a sleep vision. He got up on all fours and shook himself. Remembering that he was on a quest for meat, he sniffed the air, inhaling deeply. Nothing of particular interest in the wind right now. "Just in case I get a tova or a flattail today, I'd better get prepared." He lumbered along the shoreline and back into the forest until he came to his special tree. The trunk of this jackpine was thicker than most of those in the area. The bark was soft but the wood pulp was hard. Standing on his back legs he put both front paws against the bark. He began to pull first one paw then the other, allowing his long claws to penetrate into the wood. Pieces of bark fell, some hitting Kuru in the face. But he didn't care. He needed sharp claws for his mission. When he felt he had scraped and whetted enough, he licked the claws clean of debris, testing the trenchancy of each.

With his claws freshly honed, Kuru felt confident, he could walk a little heavier, stride with purpose. Before leaving his chosen pine, he stood up on his hind legs and rubbed his back against the roughed-up surface of the tree trunk. It not only felt good, but a little pine sap worked into his fur kept bugs away. He especially liked the sweet woodsy aroma of the pine. Now he was ready to go into the water after a flattail if necessary. Their nest was at the other end of the lake, the end near the uprights' nest. A long walk from here. So Kuru would need some nourishment on the way.

He found some rocky ground covered with moss. There were always some insects living under the moss and it was easy to turn over. A quick meal. He got busy turning over patches of the green and brown spongy moss. Within minutes he had consumed a quantity of sow bugs. Although they were not very filling, Kuru did like the crunchiness. He swallowed most of them whole but always crunched on a few. That would do for a while. He set out once again for the flattail lodge.

He began thinking about flattails. They were easy to spot and to smell when their head was gliding along on the surface of the water. He could overtake one swimming. But the problem was they would dive under. And Kuru did *not* like to swim underwater. He didn't mind paddling with his head out. In fact he was good at it. He could overtake not only a flattail but also a koda or noda[11] Underwater he could not see very well and would lose his sense of direction. Besides, paddling didn't work as well underwater. So flattails had the advantage in the water. He had to break into their water nest to capture the little ones. They were so tender, easy to swallow, and filling. Just thinking about them he began to salivate.

A distant bellowing interrupted his meditation on flattails.

"A koda. Making his presence known." His mental image instantly switched from the succulent morsel of a baby flattail to the hearty, meaty carcass of a tova. That's what he really wanted now. He took a deep breath, envisioning his fangs sinking into the soft, warm belly of a fat young tova. He breathed deeply again. "What is that odor?" He sniffed a few times. It was a familiar aroma. It took only seconds for him to recognize the scent of a noda during the coupling season. Was he imagining it? Or was it real? Yes, definitely a noda was nearby and most likely last year's tova was with her.

Kuru felt excitement and energy building. His shoulder muscles twitched. His eyes widened. Lifting his nose higher he followed the scent. It led him in the direction of the uprights' nest. It was leaving Big Lake and going along the path to Little Lake. Kuru started loping toward the path. "Noda will try to kick me and do all she can to keep me from her tova. The tova will try to

---

[11] noda = moose cow

get away, but I will take it in my jaws and run." Kuru foamed at the mouth. His breath was deep and fast, making rumblings in his throat. His mind cut off. Instinct took over. He had reached the path. He was ready to kill.

"An upright! Not a noda or a tova! An upright!" Kuru was more furious than confused. He turned his head from side to side in an effort to cope with the excess energy and rage. The upright started jumping up and down, waving poles in one hand, a shiny object in the other. Screaming noises came from its mouth.

"I will destroy it!" Kuru turned his muzzle up, lengthening it as much as possible. He opened his mouth wide and vocalized his anger and confusion. He spread his claws. He was controlled by nothing but the powerful drive to unleash his fury. He raised himself to a full standing position like the upright, making his own screaming noises. Then he attacked, running full force toward the upright. Something sharp struck the left side of his face near the eye. Kuru stood up again roaring against the stab wound. Horrible noises came from his throat to protest the deception and pain. His left eye filled with blood. He had never before felt such intense pain. The world began to spin around him. Solid in the center of it was the noda-scented upright. Kuru renewed the charge.

Rather than planning his moves, he was following some primal force within. When the upright began to run, Kuru felt more excitement and energy. The chase was a major component of his basic instinct. It took only a few bounds. He pounced, easily pushing the upright to the ground. His fangs went through flesh and bone. Upright blood was in his mouth. Kuru now felt a sense of dominance over his victim. With his nose so near the upright's neck the smell of a noda was stronger. He released his jaws. His claws began digging at the upright's back trying to find the source of the noda aroma. It was strongest near the neck and hands. The upright squirmed and screamed. Kuru went back to the grip with his teeth.

After a while the upright ceased to move. There didn't seem to be any breath going in and out. "The life force has gone from it," Kuru assumed. He licked the neck and hands where the noda scent was strong. No use. This was not a noda. There was no tova with her. Kuru turned back on the path.

"I wanted that tova!! I wanted it!! I needed it for the long sleep of the white season!" Kuru didn't go far until his anger flared up again. "I will kill that upright. I have already tasted its life's liquid." Kuru loped back to the victim, pushed it with his forepaw and sniffed the neck again. No response. Kuru put both paws on the upright's back and pounced up and down. Still no response. Snorting his frustration, he turned away again, but got no farther. "I want to hurt that upright some more because it hurt me. My face is swelling and I can't see well out of one eye! I want to make it feel pain!

Kuru returned several times to his victim until he was convinced the thing was dead and it could not harm him nor was it necessary to inflict any more damage. Besides he needed to take care of his own wound. The blood was already hardening over the left side of his face. His eye was almost shut. Kuru was in such a state that he didn't know where he was going. After a while he found himself near his den, the place he had picked out for the long sleep. Leaning against a white pine he licked his paw and swept it over the wound. It hurt. But Kuru continued cleaning. He had never been injured before. He was once bitten on a leg by a sharp-nosed bushy tail[12], but it didn't hurt like this.

When the cleaning was done to the best of his ability, Kuru decided he wanted to make sure the upright was dead. For some reason he still wasn't convinced. So, as tired as he was and partially blinded, he had to go back. He knew the woods well and had no trouble finding the path to the uprights' nest. But his victim was gone. Once again he felt betrayed and confused.

"Not dead! It's not dead! I will find that upright." No sooner had he begun to follow the upright's noda scent toward the nest than he heard the sound of the roaring bird[13] landing. That was the one creature he knew he could not subdue.

---

[12] sharp-nosed bushy tail = red fox
[13] roaring bird = floatplane

"No, I cannot go after the upright now. The roaring bird will carry it off. It brings them all in and takes them all away. But I will find the upright that hurt me. I will hunt it, I will find it, and I will kill it!" Kuru stood on all fours, his heart pounding, his jaw tight, his mind set. Blood trickled from the stab wound in his face and fell to the forest floor.

* * *

"I know where the roaring bird goes when it leaves here. A place with lots of uprights and several nests. I've been there once before. That's where my upright is. It's far to the west of my roaming lands. But I'm going." Kuru lay down near his den under his sharpening tree. He couldn't stop thinking about the false noda that hurt him. His eye was still swollen and painful but the bleeding had stopped. Now he needed a nap. He curled up. "Yes. As soon as I wake up, I will start out to find that upright. It will be a long journey. I will see and hear, and smell, and taste new things." His desire grew to take this journey not only to find the upright but also to explore his territory. The journey to kill was becoming a journey of discovery.

The next light cycle he waited until the sky light had descended and turned big and red. He headed toward it, knowing that was the right direction to reach the upright herd. He remembered their water skimmers that move so fast over the enormous lake. But he didn't fear them for he had no intention of going anywhere in the water. After all, he was not after flattails or swimmers.

'Maybe I'll find a noda with her tova on the way." Kuru ambled on, listening to the fluttering and chirping of the boreal chickadees. After a while he came out into an open space where a stream broke into streamlets that flowed into the lake, like a miniature delta, a bountiful marshland filled with fish eggs, little minnows and hatchlings.

"This is a good place to stop and feed for a while." Kuru stuck his muzzle into the cool stream. He watched little swimmers darting about then put a paw in to trap one or two. Before he could retrieve any, he heard a screaming sound. A long claw screaming sound. He immediately stood up into fighting position and spotted a female and two young cubs on the opposite bank of the stream. Her muzzle was raised, mouth open, claws poised in front of her. Kuru sized up the cubs. "One of them would make a good meaty meal or two." He lowered himself to all fours and started bounding across the stream. She met him head on, standing, roaring and screaming and showing no fear. Kuru did likewise. But his heart was not in a fight. He felt sure he could overpower her, run her off, and grab one of the cubs, both of whom had scampered up the nearest tree and were peering around the trunk, one head on each side.

"She will fight hard, give me claw scrapes and probably some bad bites. I'm already wounded, can't see out of one eye. Better settle for a few little swimmers." Kuru backed down, sidled away, moved farther downstream, and left the female to reassure her babies.

The journey continued. Kuru satisfied his hunger with some late-season berries, tree nuts, and one striped ground runner.[14] He lumbered on, his heavy footfall everywhere prompting feathered flyers to leave their branches in a hurry and express their fear and scorn from above. Kuru paid them no mind. Nothing could distract him from his mission. But something did cause him to stop. He inhaled and listened. A faintly familiar aroma and a whirring noise he hadn't heard in a long time. He kept sniffing and listening until he remembered. "Buzzers!"[15] Instinct told him to search the surrounding tree trunks for hollows. He found the nest encircled by dozens of buzzers. Kuru forced the tip of his muzzle into the nest, stuck out his tougue and pulled in a delightful mixture of buzzer larvae, the chewy stuff that encases them in tiny dens, and that sweet, thick liquid that pervades the entire nest. "So good, so good." The one food that Kuru could savor. He barely felt the pricks of their bites on his nose and ear

[14] chipmunk
[15] bees

tips. No matter. This was too good and too rare. Kuru's enjoyment of the buzzers' liquid made him feel content. Now he wanted to sleep and have visions. A cool, shady spot in a clump of chokecherry bushes was the perfect place. Besides, it was almost dark time. Although Kuru preferred to travel and hunt during the short time between the dim light and the true dark, as did most of the forest creatures, the stab wound and buzzer bites were making his whole face throb. "Best to sleep. At first light I will find something to eat and be on my way again."

At first light Kuru did encounter a small creature waddling through the brush, but it was not to become his next meal. The black furry critter with two white stripes running the length of its body stopped at Kuru's advance, stomped the ground with its front paws and hissed, warning the predator to back off. But Kuru lowered his head, stretched his neck, and took another step forward. Big mistake. The little animal turned its rear, lifted its tail, and sprayed the long claw in the face. Kuru screamed, stood up on hind legs, and desperately wiped his face with the sides of his forepaws. The smell was so atrocious it stopped him from breathing.

"Need to put my head in water!" He galloped away seeking a stream or pond. With his head in a small flattail pond he found some relief for all his ills. After a few soakings Kuru considered:

"I should have known better. A black and white sprayer[16]. This has happened to me before. But I forgot about that horrible smell. I will never again try to eat one of those things."

After another light and dark cycle, Kuru awoke to strange noises. He recognized the sound of the roaring bird and water skimmers. But there were other sounds, grinding, chugging, humming noises, and upright voices coming from a clearing just ahead. Staying within the cover of the trees, he watched and listened. He could smell uprights, lots of uprights. He could smell food, lots of food. "This is good." Standing there taking in the sights, smells, and sounds of the uprights, he knew he had reached

---

[16] Skunk

the destination of his journey. He thought and thought but Kuru could not remember why he had come to this place.

For almost the whole light cycle Kuru watched, listened, and sniffed from the safety of the tree line next to a barren strip of hard surface. No trees, no bushes, just flat, hard land that extended from water edge to as far as Kuru's good eye could see. He had never encountered anything like this before. To get to the uprights' nests he would have to cross it. As the sky light descended and grew bigger and redder all the uprights began to enter the biggest nest from which enticing food aromas wafted. Kuru acutely felt the emptiness of his stomach. He wanted something to eat and thought he might be able to find a meal over there. Following his primal urge to eat, he started across the hard, flat land.

* * *

Meredith and Mark sat in the Cinnamon Lake outpost cabin. The unmarked plastic bottle of moose estrous rested on the table in front of them.

"If only someone had labeled it, or taken it back home with them, Billy wouldn't be in the hospital." Meredith sighed.

"Billy's going to be okay, and we'll take the bottle of estrous with us and dispose of it. But the problem, the danger, is the bear. He's out there. Wounded and most probably very angry. And he has tasted human blood. I'm sure I can get a tag on him, but we can't mount a full-scale bear hunt and run the lodge."

"Can we hire some hunters? I'm sure there are quite a few who would jump at the chance to go bear hunting and get paid for it."

"I've thought about that. It might cost a fortune. It could go on for several days with no guarantee of success. You know as well as I do how extensive a bear's territory is and how elusive they are. Besides, I would hate to be putting anyone else's life at risk."

"You're right, Mark. Maybe it would be best to notify the district game warden and let them handle it. In other words, pass the buck, or rather the bear."

"I'm glad to see your sense of humor has returned, Mni Ha Ha. Now let's get this moose juice outta here."

They closed up the cabin and climbed into the Cessna. Mark turned to Meredith as she was preparing for take-off. "Lucky thing no one had requested Cinnamon Lake outpost this week. We do have four guys coming in next week. I'm sending someone over tomorrow to bear-proof the cabin as much as possible."

"I'm scared, Mark. We've just got to find that bear and the missing man." She put on her headset and pulled back on the throttle. As she flew toward the lodge, one question kept repeating in her mind. "Where is he? Where is he?"

Chapter Seven
Kenora

A refreshing breeze blew through the open window billowing the white organdy curtains. Eric lay in bed feeling its gentleness brush over his face and arms. He had slept hard, exhausted from the journey, a journey that was beginning to seem unreal. Once again he faced the unknown. He was now Terrence McElvin, a boarder in a rooming house in a Canadian city he had never heard of. How long would he be here? What will he do while waiting? What if people ask him personal questions? How will he answer? Anxiety flared up in his mind and heart. He sat up and swung his legs over the side of the bed.

"I need a hot shower," Eric said aloud, just to hear the sound of his own voice. He stumbled into the bathroom. Opening the medicine cabinet he found fresh soap, safety razor and cream, all still wrapped and packaged. He took a quick shower, shaved, brushed his hair and teeth. He didn't have much choice in what to wear.

"I need clothes, I need cash. I need to find an ATM that accepts this Terrence guy's Visa or a bank that will help me out. Although he said he would keep plenty in this account, I can't continue to use Alan's money. I need something to do. I need a job." Once Eric had assessed his urgent needs, he went to take care of the most pressing: he went for coffee.

Downstairs he found a steaming coffee urn, a pitcher of cream, a sugar bowl, a few mugs, and a basket of warm breakfast muffins on the kitchen counter. He poured himself some coffee and picked up a folded note labeled "Terrence." He unfolded and read.

Good Morning, Terrence,

I trust you slept well and found everything to your liking. Your vehicle keys are hanging on the peg board above my desk in the parlor along with a key ring with two keys: one for your room and one for the front door. House rules are simple: I put a deadbolt on at midnight, so I guess you might say it's your curfew. No smoking inside, no guests in your room. You may entertain them in the parlor. Dinner is served at 7:00 for those who have paid for partial board, like you.
See you this evening. Have a pleasant day!

Margie

P.S. There is a map of Kenora in the desk drawer. You are welcome to borrow it to get oriented.

Eric chose a cranberry-walnut muffin and sat down at the table to finish his coffee. He also finished the muffin and eyed the basket, but resisted. A wave of guilt and shame spread over him. "Here I am enjoying breakfast when Sandy is buried—what's left of her after the autopsy—and Becca doesn't know anything. If only I could go back to that moment in the kitchen when Sandy was chopping vegetables for a salad. If only she hadn't cut her finger so bad. If only I hadn't grabbed her hand and wrapped it in my shirttail. If I hadn't worked so late that night. So many ifs. I should have taken her on that trip to Paris she always wanted." Eric propped an elbow on the table and put his forehead in the palm of his hand. He sat thinking and hurting, feeling both guilty and innocent. Like perpetrator and victim. Most of all he felt helpless. "All I can do is stick to Alan's plan and wait and hope they find the killer."

But in reality Eric had things to do in mind. He put his mug in the sink where he noticed several others, took the house keys off the peg board, and found the map in the desk drawer. He went back upstairs, closed the window, and locked his room door. Before leaving Margie's he studied the map. He decided to use his legs rather than wheels, explore the downtown on foot since according to the map the rooming house was centrally located. He walked to the nearest thoroughfare, noticed the sign "Second Street," and turned south toward the waterfront. "First thing: I want to find out the name of the huge body of water this town is laid out on. Whoever I ask will think I'm either crazy or stupid. Then an ATM or a bank. Then lunch. Maybe a hot dog and a beer."

He went past a number of quaint old homes, most of them well maintained, a few needing new paint and the lawn mowed. *I could cut grass for cash. Or paint houses.* Traffic on this main thoroughfare was not light, but there was a cement sidewalk. Not many pedestrians. Little by little residential gave way to commercial. A small house converted to a hair styling salon, another to an insurance agency. An office plaza, an eyeglass store. In the distance Eric could see the lake. He passed a bar-restaurant with a glass front and umbrella tables and chairs out on a small terrace. He watched employees busily preparing for the lunch crowd. "*KNK Brewing Company.* I'll have to keep this place in mind—if and when I get some cash."

Passing more small shops and a Greek restaurant, he noticed he was approaching the corner where a large historic building stood. It looked like it dated from the late nineteenth century. A sign painted on the street side read *Kenricia Hotel.* The old hotel had been artfully restored. "I'd like to see inside one of these days." Eric appreciated repaired and restored things. Afterall, that's what he did for a living. The Kenricia Hotel sat at the corner of Second Street and a street which paralleled the waterfront, which he later learned was Main Street. Second Street apparently ended but a short driveway continued down to a dock where a few float planes were moored. A man in an army-green T-shirt and well-worn jeans was loading boxes onto a large flat dolly.

"Excuse me. Sorry to bother you, but could you tell me the name of this lake?"

The man stood up and turned to see who had spoken.

"Well, nobody has ever asked me *that* question before! I guess you've never been in the area."

"You're right. And yes, it is an ignorant question, but I'd like to know."

"Lake of the Woods. Lower part is in the USA. It's over 100 kilometers long and wide with lots of islands and lots of fish. We have championship bass and walleye tournaments. You a fisherman?"

"I've done some fishing, but I'm not very good at it. I'd like to get better. And I'd like to teach my daughter to enjoy fishing in the wilderness."

"Take her up to one of my outposts." He extended a hand. "Kevin Walsten. I operate Walsten Outposts right off this dock."

"Eri—Terrence McElvin." Eric shook his hand. The man had a good firm grip and an honest face. Eric liked him right away.

"Check out my website. Be glad to have you and your wife and daughter." He returned to his loading.

You and your wife. . . . The words singed inside. Eric closed his eyes and took a deep breath. He looked out at the lake. *Lower part is in the USA.* Homesickness and loneliness were hard to deal with especially when added to the fear of imprisonment and possibly lethal injection. He walked out farther onto the dock past the floatplanes. The wind off the lake was invigorating and helped ease the pain and anxiety. He decided to continue his walk through the center of town.

Main Street sat on a rise that paralleled the lake front. There were restaurants spread out below with outdoor dining. Eric passed a fine-dining restaurant built of large cut stones. It occupied a corner on the intersection of Second Street and Main Street. "A place for special occasions," Eric thought. He turned onto Main Street and walked by a number of shops and restaurants. An ATM booth outside the Royal Bank of Canada swallowed his Visa and spat it back out along with a handful of Canadian twenty-dollar bills. It felt good to have cash in his pocket. Added a little security to his precarious existence. Between buildings he could see a cruise boat. Signs advertised lake cruises and a sunset dinner cruise aboard the MS Kenora. "Sandy would enjoy that." When he reached the point where Main Street started to curve around a bay, he stopped in front of a remarkable old historic-looking building which a sign identified as City Hall. Constructed entirely of red brick with a square clock tower on one side. All the doors and windows were arched and topped by large gray-white cut stones similar to those of the restaurant. It stood like a proud guardian of the little town.

Eric thought about going inside, but his stomach told him that his breakfast muffin was spent. So he headed back to the KNK Brewery. It wasn't a short walk and by the time he got there he was starving. Even though he was happy to have the twenties in his pocket, he was relieved to see the Visa emblem on the glass door as he entered. At the counter he looked over the menu. Lots of creative choices. But he stuck with his hot dog and beer which he took to a table outside. He surveyed the other customers on the terrace, mostly young and single, then watched pedestrians pass by. His attention was soon drawn to the gas station across the street. *Abbott's Automotive Service* with three bays attached. But what caught his eye was the collapsible wooden sign in front of one of the bays. *Mechanic wanted.* A truck sat in the other bay, the hood up, and the bottom half of a person visible in front of the vehicle. Eric sipped on his beer mustering the courage to do what he knew he couldn't resist. He left the beer mug on the table, tossed his trash in a bin by the door, and crossed Second Street.

"Ford Ranchero 1979. Last of the line. Great ol' pickup." Eric commented while watching the top half of the person come out from under the hood. "Nicely restored. I like the bright blue color and the white stripes running from back taillights to front windshield along the top of the truck walls and slope."

"Yeah. She's beautiful, but she won't run. You come to apply for the job?"

"Mainly came over to see the Ranchero. But I'd also like to know more about the job. Name's Terrence McElvin." Eric extended a hand. In spite of the nerves he got the name right.

"Charlie Abbott." He returned the handshake. Eric noticed the name embroidered on his gray and red uniform. "Had a darn good mechanic but had to let him go. Totally unreliable. Never knew when he was going to show up. And then if he was sober. I own the station and the shop but I'm not much at auto repair. I depend on a good mechanic. What's your story?"

"I don't really have a story. Been working on cars since I was eight years old. In high school I was the 'go to' guy for anybody who owned a car and needed help. Been doing it ever since. I'm an ASE certified master mechanic."

"You took all those tests?"

"I did."

"Think you might be able to get this Ford going?"

"I can give it a try. What's it doing?"

"Weird problem. It cranks over but just won't fire. Should have plenty of gas I just filled it."

Eric stuck his head under the Ranchero's hood. Charlie stood back. Eric went through the standard check of wiring connections, mainly the wires to the coil and the spark plug wires to be sure there was nothing obvious preventing a spark. The wires all looked good. Then he had a hunch. He slid under the front of the Ranchero.

"Could I have, let's see, is that a seven-sixteenths? Or just an adjustable wrench to make it easy?" Charlie reached into a tool stand, handed Eric the wrench. Eric went to work tightening the bolts holding the fuel pump then came out from under the vehicle.

"Try starting her up now."

Charlie obliged and got into the car. At first it cranked and cranked but did not fire. Charlie looked at Eric who smiled and said "Try again." This time with one turnover of the engine she started purring. He gave a long low whistle. "What the heck did you do? I've been trying everything I know all morning. Beginning to think she needed some serious parts replacement."

"Some rough terrain must have loosened the fuel pump so much that the lever couldn't reach the cam that actuates it. I also noticed that the fuel line has a ding in it and should be replaced.

And while you are at it, you could replace the fuel filter. But she's okay for now.

"Could you do that work?"

"No problem."

"Will you take the job?

"It may be a possibility."

"I tell you what. Come on into the office and we'll do the paperwork. You're an American so you'll need a Visa or a work permit." Do you have a Canadian bank account for monthly direct deposit?"

"Look, Mr. Abbott. On second thought, I don't think we can do this. I would need to be paid in cash, preferably weekly. No paperwork. Sorry to have bothered you. Glad I could help you out with the Ford." Eric started out the bay.

"Wait, Terrence. I think we can work this out. I get it. You have to stay under the radar. For whatever reason. That's your business. I need a mechanic, you need work and money. Why don't we try it for a week? If it works out, fine. If not, no harm done. Nobody needs to know anything. It'll be just between you and me."

Eric turned back and smiled. "That sounds like a plan, Mr. Abbott."

"Call me Charlie."

They shook hands again.

"You staying at Margie's?"

"That's right."

"Can't do any better than that. She's tops around here. Everybody knows her and loves her."

"Say, Charlie, can you direct me to a men's clothing store?"

"Well, right out the door is a nice, clean second-hand place. Or you can go down Second to Chipman to First and you'll find a wholesale clothing store. Then there's always North Face on Main Street if you want to spend some serious money."

Thanks. I'll check them out."

* * *

On the walk back to Margie's Eric carried two bags of clothes. T-shirts and sweatshirts and a pair of jeans from the used clothing store and some comfortable khaki pants, a shirt, and a jacket from the wholesale outlet. That would do for now. More needs taken care of. Yet nothing eased his mind. He worried that taking the job may be too risky. What if Charlie spills the beans about him to a friend or family member? Gut instinct told him that he could trust the boss to keep his mouth completely shut. But people will ask about the new mechanic. What will he say? Now Eric had the burden of secrecy more than ever. Up at Cinnamon Lake with Billy and Jake there was little or no personal talk, no real need to dissemble. Up there he was off the grid. But now ....

He sat on a little stone wall that banked up against a front lawn. The loss, the grief, the uncertainty of his future, the phony life he was carving out here in Kenora, and the overwhelming loneliness weighed him down, made him feel like he was trying to walk into a wind tunnel blowing full blast at him. Breathing was hard. Eric felt a terrible need to be truthful with someone. "No. Can't. Too dangerous. Alan said 'Don't tell anyone anything.'" Yet he had mentioned his daughter to the outfitter on the dock and he had told Charlie he was an ASE master mechanic. Could that give away his true identity? It was all too much for his brain. He gathered his packages and walked head down looking at the sidewalk until he found himself in front of the yellow and white house with the sign that read *Margie's Rooms and Meals.*

The front door key worked smoothly. He entered the hall and noticed Margie at her desk in the parlor. She looked up from her paperwork, peering over her perched glasses.

"Good afternoon, Mr. McElvin. Have you had a good day in our little town?"

"Yes, I have. I met some pleasant citizens, had a nice lunch, and saw some amazing old buildings."

"I'm glad. May I ask who the 'pleasant citizens' were?"

Eric went into the parlor, put his bags of clothing down, and sat on the couch. "On the waterfront I met an outfitter named Kevin Walsten and then a gas station owner, Charlie Abbott."

"Well, you have made the acquaintance of two of Kenora's finest. Kevin and his lovely wife are good friends and they are hard workers. His outposts are beautiful and he is one of Canada's best bushpilots. And I've known Charlie all my life. We went to school together.

"Charlie needs a mechanic and offered me the job."

"Really? Now that is a surprise. Charlie is very particular about his mechanics. You must be very good at it. I take it you're pleased."

"We'll see how it goes." Eric stood to go to his room.

"Don't forget. Supper is at seven."

"I'll be there."

Eric found his bed made and the bathroom freshly cleaned. He put his bags down in the TV chair, unlaced and pulled off his boots, then stretched out on the bed.

"I forgot to get some new shoes. These fishing boots are a mess from that grueling trek from Cinnamon to Kenora. Might be hard to find the right size at the thrift shop." Mulling over the kind of shoes to buy and where to get them became soporific. He was standing on the dock in Kenora watching a duck swimming around. The duck flew up onto the dock and stood next to him. One of its legs was wrapped in duct tape.

Something was knocking, tapping.

"Mr. McElvin. . . .Mr. McElvin. You have a visitor. He's waiting in the parlor."

Eric's eyes popped full open.

* * *

The aroma of pot roast met Charlie when he entered the back door.

"Smells good, Honey." He found his wife setting out plates on the little kitchen table.

Hugging her from behind he kissed the back of her neck.

"What brought that on? You must be in your happy-day mood."

'I most certainly am!" He opened the oven to inspect the contents. "I hired a new mechanic today. He really seems to know his stuff. Fixed that Ford truck." Charlie sat down at his usual place, stuck a napkin in his lap, and watched his wife put a moose roast, boiled potatoes, and a crispy-looking salad on the table. "He just walked into the shop out of nowhere. He's not Canadian. American." He stabbed a potato. "Funny thing, though, he didn't want the job if it involved any official paperwork. Wants to be paid weekly. In cash. He must be in some sort of legal trouble in the States."

"Probably a dead-beat dad. Running from child support payments. That's what a lot of them do. Change their ID and leave the country."

"Maybe you're right, but he didn't strike me as that kind. Something about him seemed a little sad. But I tell you he knows cars. Took him about five minutes to find the problem and fix it. I'd been working at it all morning. Nance, this roast is DE-licious." He chewed for a while. "Anyway, we're going to try it for a week to see how it goes."

"If you decide to keep him on after the trial week, invite him over for dinner. A few glasses of wine and I'll bet he'll slip up and reveal what he's hiding."

"If we blow his cover, I'll lose my mechanic. Besides, he trusts me. I appreciate that."

 Charlie illustrated his point by waving around a piece of meat on his fork.

"Still, I sure would like to know who he really is." Nancy didn't say another word at dinner.

Chapter Eight
At the Lodge

Weather conditions at Baldwin Lake Lodge had been ideal for the past two weeks. Moderately warm days with cool nights. Light winds had made the crossing of the big lake easy rendering all the fisheries of the northern sections accessible. The guests were taking full advantage, coming in each day with record numbers of trophy-sized northern pike, walleye and even a few lake trout despite that species' retreat to deeper, colder water. But weather reports were predicting a change. A drop in temperature with rain and storm cells moving in from the northwest. Most of the fishermen who were guests at the lodge were pretty intrepid. Bad weather simply meant better fishing, according to the old saying, "Wind from the East fish bite least. Wind from the West fish bite best." They would don their hooded Gortex rain suits and brave the elements in search of more and bigger fish.

Meredith and Mark, also clad in rain suits when necessary, always went to the boat dock each morning to see off the fishermen and fisherwomen and guides. It would be a long but exciting day for all of them. Guests would sit in the boats while the guides waited for the magic moment when synchronized watches read eight o'clock, time to head out. Meredith loved to watch the boats take off, spreading out to the four winds, their separating wakes carving long graceful arcs on the surface of the water. All her childhood summers were spent here. One morning she found a half-starved wolf pup, raised him to adulthood, then released him back into the wild. Going into the wilderness to reunite with her wolf, she met an Ojibwe who, years later, would become her husband. She learned to fly the float plane and got her pilot's license right here on Baldwin Lake. This was home, her home in Nature. Over the years she had observed so much wildlife and displays of Nature, all right here. Her high school classmates could never understand why she didn't care for drinking, drugs, and dancing parties, why she wasn't caught up in social media interaction, or why she in no way wanted to sleep around. She may not have been the most popular girl at school, but she had her friends, friends who shared her passion for the outdoors. And she had Mark, and a future with him. Her mother and Bobby had opened a huge door for the two of them by handing them the reins of Baldwin Lake. Life was good. With one exception: she could not stop thinking about the Cinnamon Lake bear. "It's still out there," she kept reminding herself. And so is the missing man.

SAR had called off both ground and air search for the missing man. Although no clothing or body parts had been found, everyone was assuming that he was a fatal victim of the bear. The body, what would be left of it, was somewhere deep within the density of the taiga. The media had lost interest, no more TV news spots, no newspaper articles. One thing puzzled Meredith: why wasn't his family concerned? Not a peep out of them. Shouldn't they be here looking for their lost loved one? Shouldn't they be bombarding us with questions? Was he such a loner that he had no family or friends? What about his job? His coworkers? She would talk with Mark, Karen, and Bobby about this. They really needed to find out who he was (or is), other than just an American named Terrence McElvin from the Chicago area.

She sat at the computer in the lodge office reading email. Mark was at his desk dealing with finances. While the guests were out fishing, the two couples had the place to themselves. Perfect time to take care of business. When boats came in for the day, all four of them liked to mingle and chat. After all the guests had settled in their cabins for the night, the couples retreated to their own spaces. Karen and Bobby had built their own cabin while Meredith and Mark occupied the owners' quarters in the back part of the main building, the same living quarters she shared with her mother and Bobby through her childhood and young adulthood.

"Hey, Mark. Here's an email from Billy's wife. You'll want to check it out."

Mark opened an envelope from a pile on his desk without looking up "Is he still in the hospital?"

"I'll read you the email."

Dear Baldwin Lake Lodge Managers,

First let me thank you for visiting my husband in the hospital. He really appreciates your taking time out of your busy schedule up at Baldwin Lake to come down here to check on him. Doctors say his recovery is progressing nicely, but he will need a few more days of rest and observation in the hospital. He wants you to know that in no way does he hold you responsible for what happened to him. He takes full blame for smearing himself with an unknown liquid which he has learned was moose estrous. Nor does he blame the bear which was acting by instinct. He will be forever grateful to you for saving his life.

He asked me to write this expression of gratitude but also to tell you that he would like to come back next year. He and Jake Barnes will be together again. There will also be a third party. Which brings me to the other reason for writing: Have they found Terrence? Billy worries much more about him than about his own condition. He remembered one thing that might help locate his family. Terrence once mentioned his daughter. Billy thinks her name is Becky, or Betty or Bella, something like that. Otherwise all he knows is his last name McElvin.

I would like to add one question of my own. Has anything been done about the bear? Has it been taken down? Or is it still free to attack again? I'm sure you are doing everything you can to prevent this from happening again, but I know that when a person goes into the wild they take their chances. I look forward to hearing from you when you get a moment.

With deep heartfelt thanks,

Sarah Stiles

P.S. We appreciate the refund. It will help with some of the medical expenses not covered by insurance.

"Nice to get mail like that, huh, Sweetheart? They could have taken a completely different attitude toward us." Mark went back to his paperwork.

"Should we inform the authorities that Terrence has a daughter named Becky?"

"I don't see how that will help them, but you never know."

"Is that a yes or a no?"

"It's a 'you-do-what-you-think-best' answer." Mark gave her a mocking smile that turned into a real one.

Meredith turned back to the computer.

"Here's one from Jake. Wanna hear it?"

"Go ahead, Madame Secretary."

Hi Mark and Meredith,

Billy and I have been texting, and we both remember that Terrence mentioned his daughter Becky or Bekka. Could be short for Rebekka. I read that Canadian authorities are trying to locate his family and thought this little tidbit might help. If I think of anything else I'll let you know. BTW, Billy and I both want to come back to Cinnamon next year. Maybe earlier in the summer—June? Let me know if the outpost is available. People think we are crazy, but lightening doesn't strike twice in the same place, right? And we will be sure to bring insect spray! And thanks for getting me out of that tree!

Jake Barnes

"We do have wonderful clientele, don't we?"

"Thanks to your mother and Bobby who ran this place so flawlessly. We're not off to a great start."

"I think we are." Meredith left her seat, went behind Mark, put her hands on his shoulders and gave him a nuzzling kiss on one cheek then the other.

Mark reached up and squeezed one of her hands. "Hold that thought until bedtime."

* * *

Karen and Bobby motored in about four, having spent the day fun fishing and just enjoying a day on the lake complete with shore lunch. They took full advantage of their leisure time now that Meredith and Mark were managing the camp.

"Well, here come the lovebirds." Meredith poured two Crown-Royals-on-the-rocks while the older couple settled in at the bar. "How was the fishing today? Who caught the biggest fish?"

"Your Mom landed a 37-inch pike …."

"And right after that Bobby showed me up with a 38 incher. No trophies. But we had a great time. Saw a mink running along the shore and got a glimpse of a moose drinking in Beaver Creek."

"You two always have fun no matter what you do."

"And what have you kids been up to today?" Bobby swirled his glass to stir the drink.

Meredith leaned over the counter in front of her stepfather. "Work!" she said with a teasing pout.

"Any news about the McElvin guy? Has he been reunited with his family?" Karen sat her glass aside. "It seems that nobody knows anything about him." Mark joined his wife behind the bar. "Except that he has a daughter possibly named Rebecca. We learned that from Billy and Jake via email."

"Has anyone Googled him?" Bobby asked.

"I did. But nothing." Meredith added. "I found a guy named Terrence McElvene, spelled differently, who died four years ago at age eighty-seven. We know he's from the Chicago area. But that hasn't helped."

"Do you suppose he's using an alias?" Karen's question silenced the group for a few minutes.

"I have a friend in the police department in Winnipeg. I'll ask him how they track down suspects who have gone incognito. You know, it's not that unusual for an escapee from prison to get across the border and hide out in Canada," Bobby said.

"What are we now? Baldwin Lake Private Investigators?"

At Meredith's facetious remark, they heard the sound of exhausted but excited guests clomping up the front steps, sliding the glass door open, and filing into the dining hall.

"Let's clear the bar," Karen suggested.

"And get ready to hear some fish tales," Mark added, pulling beers out of the ice.

"Mama, will you check with the cook to make sure she's ready to serve dinner?"

Just as Meredith spoke, the chef came out of the kitchen with two plates of appetizers which she placed on the bar. Deviled eggs and spinach balls on one, vegetable dip on the other. She was semi-retired from years of being head chef at a gourmet restaurant in downtown Winnipeg. The lodge was lucky to secure her. The guests devoured her delectable dishes and lauded her culinary skills.

It seems that we are asking a lot of questions but not getting any answers, Meredith thought as she circulated among the tables listening to the fishermen tell their tales or comment on the food.

A commotion at a table across the room by a window drew everyone's attention. Guests left their seats and hurried over to the windows on that side to see for themselves what had caused such a stir.

"It's a bear! A black bear!" someone called out. Meredith rushed into the office which was on that side of the building.

"What's all the fuss about?" Mark asked her.

"A bear has wandered into the camp. We have to do something quick."

Mark rushed into the tackle shop across the hall, grabbed a can of bear spray off the shelf and dashed out the back door. Once outside he stood tall, walked slowly and deliberately toward the animal. He stopped about fifteen feet away and stood still.

Meredith watched from the office window, heart pumping. The guests were enjoying the incident as if it were dinner theater. Meredith had seen Mark face off with a bear once before when they were together in the wilderness the first time, so she knew what to expect. "He will win the standoff." Still, she feared for his safety. She noticed that the bear spray was in a back pocket of his jeans, not in his hand. She could see his mouth moving and knew he was speaking to brother bear in his native language. The bear reared up on hind legs and Meredith's heart seemed to stop. But he came back down on all fours right away. Mark took several steps forward. The bear made a warning lunge at him. Mark didn't flinch, but continued to speak, showing no fear. At this point Meredith resorted to her Christian heritage and began to pray. "Lord, please give Mark power over the bear. Please don't let the bear attack!"

Although she had faith in the power of prayer, she opened the closet and took out a rifle, a box of shells, and loaded the weapon. She positioned herself at the window with a clear shot at the bear. "Just in case," she told herself while trying to control her hands. The bear threw back his head, held his muzzle high and let out a noise that sounded more like a bellow than a growl. Meredith put her index finger on the trigger and clenched her jaw. Perspiration beaded on her forehead and upper lip.

Mark continued to speak slowly and firmly. The bear began to look around, one side and then the other. "He's looking for a safe way out. Go on, bear, take off. I don't want to shoot you but I'm certainly not going to let you hurt my husband!" Although she knew the bear could not hear her, she felt she was communicating.

Meredith's faith in Mark, or in prayer, or in the rifle paid off. The bear turned around and loped back out toward the airstrip and the woods beyond. Meredith let out the breath she didn't realize she had been holding.

Applause broke out in the dining hall. The guests, who had fallen silent during the standoff, were now talking in excited rhythms. Meredith lowered the gun to her side and slid into the desk chair waiting for Mark to come back in. When he did, Meredith decided to play it cool.

"I see you haven't lost your touch."

"Bears will be bears. Hey, what's with the rifle?"

"Let's just say I had your back."

"Come here. I could use a hug!"

Meredith replaced the rifle then threw her arms around her husband's neck. They held on to each other until the fear and pumping hearts subsided.

"Thanks, Mini Ha Ha."

"You're welcome, Nagweyaab[17]. You know, the guests really enjoyed the show. You received a standing ovation."

"That's one role I never want to play again."

"Mark, Ojibwe warrior, commander of bears."

Karen appeared at the office door. "Mark, are you crazy? Confronting that bear without a weapon? I don't want my daughter to become a widow at twenty-three."

"I had bear spray in my pocket. And my partner here had me covered—with a rifle."

"Well that's good to know. We once had a bear enter the camp, but we drove it away by banging pots and pans together, yelling, and making as much noise as possible."

"That'll work."

"I think we need to go out and reassure the guests. I'm sure many of them are feeling uneasy." Karen led the way. Mark put his arm around his wife's shoulders and the two followed Karen into the dining hall where Bobby was manning a very busy bar. Mark was bombarded with questions and gratuitous comments.

What did you say to that bear?
Do you often have bears come into the lodge grounds?
What do you think he wanted? Food?
Do you leave scraps out for the wildlife?
Has a moose ever come to the dining hall?
 Boy, that took some guts to face that bear one-on-one like that!
I bet you had a gun in your belt!
 I would've killed that beast!

---

[17] Mark's Ojibwe name meaning "rainbow"

I got the whole thing on video. Do you want a copy? I'm gonna post it on Facebook.

Meredith watched Mark navigate the room with grace and humility. Little by little the excitement subsided and the novelty faded. Guests left for their cozy cabins and soft warm beds. The all-day fishing exhilaration, the evening bear adventure, and a full dinner had prepared them for quick access to dreamland.

Meredith was fatigued, too. She escaped to their living quarters, took a hot shower, put on her pj's, and slipped into bed. Mark attended to some last-minute arrangements and instructions for the guides before joining his wife.

"Don't you dare say the word 'b – e – a – r' to me." Meredith rolled on her side away from Mark. Her husband was silent. Meredith rolled back over.

"What? I know you have something to say."

"Are you ready for this?"

"What? Tell me."

"You were probably too far away to notice, but as I stood there facing the, uh, animal, I saw that he had an ugly wound just below his left eye. Like he had been stabbed—perhaps with a filet knife."

* * *

To help their sleuth work, Meredith subscribed to the online Chicago Tribune. Since Billy and Jake were from the Windy City, she figured Terrence was, too. She hoped to turn up an article about a man who disappeared, a man fleeing alimony and child support, or a worse crime. But if he were using an alias, how could she connect the name in the paper with the name Terrence? She scrolled and read, scrolled and read the daily paper going back several weeks until she grew dizzy. She was about to call it a night when a short article seemed to jump out at her.

Murder Suspect Disappears.

A person of interest in a recent murder case has disappeared from his home in Chicago. Police fear he may have left the state or country to avoid being indicted. He is wanted in connection with the brutal slaying of his wife, Sandra Sanders. The husband has not been seen or heard in over three weeks. The CPD asks that you contact them immediately if you know the whereabouts of the fugitive.

A photo was printed beside the article. Meredith hit *Copy* twice.

"I'll send a copy to Billy and one to Jake. It's a longshot, but just maybe this could be our missing man. A murder suspect. Better than being dinner for a hungry bear."

Chapter Nine
Kuru

Kuru stopped when he saw the upright come out of its huge nest. It didn't seem to have a firestick. The upright came to a standstill facing Kuru. It opened its mouth and began saying something, speaking with calm but firm authority. Kuru sensed it was a warning, an ancient and respectful warning. "I am me and you are you. We are brothers, not enemies. You will acknowledge my territory and I will acknowledge yours. I do not wish to harm you, but I will protect my own just as you will protect yours." Kuru did realize that he had invaded the upright's territory and he was greatly outnumbered here. Rather than turn tail and run, Kuru issued a warning of his own. He stood up, snarled, and made a false charge at the upright. The upright was not fooled. He stood his ground and repeated his warning.

Kuru looked one way then another, hoping to find an easy path to take. He decided his best course of action was to turn slowly and go back the way he came. He was not afraid of the upright. In fact, he admired the honorable way it behaved. It could have come out with a firestick and taken Kuru's life force. Instead, it gave him a chance to leave with dignity. The way all creatures should treat each other. Kill only when necessary for food and to protect your own.

When he reached the flat surface, Kuru hesitated. The forest and the way home lay on the other side just ahead of him. But the flat surface seemed to lead somewhere.

"I've come a long way. I should see what's here other than the uprights' nests." Besides, Kuru was hungry and something told him he would find food if he followed this way. It was long and wide and led away from any harm the uprights might inflict. So Kuru made up his mind to see where this path would take him.

The small stones that made up the surface were sharp and tore at his pawpads, but he barely noticed. He was on his way to adventure and food.

The wide path led past the upright area until no more of the nests, large or small, could be seen. Tall white pines and silver-green-leafed poplars lined the sides of the path, forming what seemed like a protective wall to Kuru. He didn't fear the uprights themselves, but he did fear their firesticks. They made him feel vulnerable. So it was good to distance himself from them. Once away from their territory, he felt strong and invincible again.

Immersed in the forest world he heard and inhaled the familiar sounds and smells of that world. He could hear the loud resonant drumming of the long-beaked red-crested pecker and envisioned a climb up the tree to the large bird's nest hole, reaching in with a paw and pulling out the crunchy eggs that he so enjoyed snacking on. Now the season is late. The eggs will have become little chicks that have already flown away.

Kuru could smell water and discovered a small pond at the end of the wide path. When he went to take a drink, he stepped what he thought was a round stone. But head and legs came out of the stone and pushed its way into the water.

"That is a strange creature. He carries his nest with him everywhere and hides in it. It's impossible to dig him out unless I can get him on his back. Which is not always easy."

Kuru satisfied his thirst and left the hard-shell alone. He was at the end of the wide path but found that a smaller earth path about three long-claws wide led off to one side. Much easier on the pawpads. The wind picked up and blew down the earth path carrying with it the odor of food. Upright food. Kuru had smelled it many times near the uprights nest in his territory and again at the large nest where he encountered the upright.

"I will soon have something to eat." The thought gave Kuru strength to tramp a little faster and courage to face more uprights if necessary. The farther he went, the stronger the aroma. But wait! The odor of food mingled with another smell, a familiar but startling smell. "There is another long-claw at the food. I may have to fight if I want to eat." Kuru detected the aroma of a ringtail, large hissing squeakers, and other small creatures. This was quite confusing to him. He wanted to find out what was going on. Before long he heard chewing, crunching, bumping, and crackling noises. The odor of uprights' food was overwhelming. Then Kuru came upon the most amazing and confounding site he had ever seen. In a large clearing there was uprights' food in various containers large and small. Some of the containers had been knocked over and the food contends lying around covering the forest floor. But what most astonished Kuru was the fact that there were more long-claws than he had paws. Some were standing on back legs feeding with their paws, others had their heads buried in large containers. There were large squeakers hopping about, a ringtail, and other creatures all feasting. Even some young long-claws were feeding themselves from the abundance. Black dead-eaters sat in the trees, occasionally swooping down for a morsel.

As Kuru studied the scene, the shock abated, and he reasoned.

"They don't have to hunt or fight for their food. It's all here for them provided by the uprights. The long-claws even tolerate each other."

His wonderment was interrupted by a loud whirring sound. It was drawing closer. Kuru took refuge behind a clump of dense chokeberry bushes. None of the other long-claws seemed concerned.

"It sounds like a water skimmer. But that's impossible. This is dry ground." He peered through the bushes. A large bug-like creature stopped in front of the food site. It had a head and a flat body. It just stood there making the humming noise. Then an upright came out of the head, went to the flat body, pulled out two bundles and walked a short way into the food area. He threw the bundles down, walked back to the big bug-like thing, and got into the head. The bug then made a wide swing around and went back the way it had come.

Kuru's nose told him there was more food in the bundles. He listened to make sure the bug was not coming back before making a move. When he felt it was safe, he approached the bundles. With one swipe of a paw he tore one open. He was right. More food. Kuru stuck his head in and began to eat things he had never tasted before. Strange, wonderful flavors. Mixed in with the food were lots of inedible items. But that didn't bother Kuru. He was soon able to detect the difference and hastily engulf the edible.

"This is great! There is so much to eat here!" And so Kuru ate, and ate, and ate. After a while his belly felt good and full and he longed for a nap. "Not too far from here." He knew his hunger would come back and this endless supply of food would take care of that. Kuru thought he might be living in a dream. Food always available. Ready and waiting. No wonder the other long-claws don't fight with each other. There is no need to.

Wandering around the nearby forest, he found a spot behind a pile of fallen trees, lay down, and promptly fell asleep. He hadn't slept long when he was awakened by pains in the middle of his body. He felt sick. Before he knew what was happening, he emptied the contents of his stomach right where he lay. He coughed. More came up. Again and again until only clear liquid was being expelled. Then he began to feel better. He moved away, found a new spot and settled down. "I must not eat so much of the upright food." Kuru always paid attention to his instincts. So he controlled himself when he went back to the food.

At first light he was back. There were fewer long-claws this early. Kuru decided to try another section of the feeding ground where he might find something of a different flavor. Scarcely had he pushed his head into a container when he heard a loud screaming behind him. He turned to find a long-claw up on back legs, muzzle in the air, bellowing in a fury. Its vocalizations and body movements communicated quite clearly. "You have usurped my place in the feeding ground. Go back to your own spot. I don't want to fight but I will." Now the other long-claws could hear. They looked over at the two of them but didn't stop chewing and swallowing. Kuru was amazed.

"They each have their place and are protective of it. Each respects the other's feeding territory, even though it's just a little area not much bigger than a flattail's nest. That and somewhere to sleep. That is all of the forest they need." Easy meals. Kuru was all for it. He had found his little corner of the feeding ground, and he should keep to that. He had learned some lessons: Don't eat too much at one time. Don't eat in another's place. Don't get involved in another's quarrel. Don't run from the big bug that brings the food. Stay away from the uprights' nests. Kuru was willing to abide by these precepts in order to live this new lifestyle where all is effortless and sure.

Kuru did not protest. He simply moved back to his original place, and all was well. Heads went back down into the discarded foodstuffs and the large squeakers continued to skulk around, hissing at each other, and carrying off large chunks of goods.

During the early dark cycle Kuru could not sleep. This was usually his time to prowl, to look for dead swimmers at water's edge, to snap up dark-time crawlers, to hear the winds change, to sense the cooling of the air, to watch the swirling lights in the sky. He was restless, impatient for the light cycle to come and along with it, the big bug with new food. That's all he could think about.

When finally the light came, Kuru made for the feeding ground. He could hear other long-claws heading toward it, too. With extraordinary self-control, each went to its own space—no quarrels, no vociferations. Even the young ones had their own place and did not venture into any other. Kuru was one of them now. He ate happily day after day, minding his own business. He had one problem: the dark time restlessness was intensifying. He tried to prowl and hunt, but he just wasn't hungry. Nothing was driving him, nothing compelled him. And so he sat, listening and watching, uneasy. Even the winds offered no respite from the sameness. Wailing loons echoed his emptiness. During one dark cycle he had thoughts of going back to the uprights' nests. Why, he didn't know.

One early light time he simply could not make himself go to the feeding ground even though he was hungry. Instead he wandered out from his sleep place, turned over a log, and lapped in a mouthful of little white crawlers. They tasted so good. No, they were not very filling, but that didn't matter. For a moment he felt content. But the attraction of the feeding ground was too strong. Before long, Kuru again found himself with his head in a container, consuming whatever was there and listening eagerly for the arrival of the big bug.

From time to time he would stop to rest and just chew for a while. He watched the ringtails checking for food droppings in first one place then another, climbing in and out of containers. The sight of one would usually trigger a chase, a pounce, and a meal. Looking around at the long-claws, he did not see one whose interest was piqued. Neither was his own. He thought about that while studying the bushy black tail with its fine white rings hanging out of a near-by receptacle. The whirring roar of the big bug cut short his musings. Kuru, like the other long-claws, had learned to ignore the primal fear of the unknown. He did not abandon his spot but waited for the throwing of new bundles. After the upright had discarded all the bundles from the body of the big bug, the upright lingered in the food area. Kuru stood up and pricked up his ears. The upright seem to be looking directly at him.

As light was fading, Kuru sat in his sleeping place and watched the round red skylight slowly disappearing. He was so full he became drowsy. Images of tails with rings protruding from containers floated around in his mind. He put his head down on his front paws and listened to the loon crying. He closed his eyes and slept.

Light and dark cycles came and went. Kuru's routine did not change. It wasn't necessary. He had all he needed without effort. Fill up at the feeding ground, go to relieve himself and take a nap, then back to the feeding ground. An occasional protest arose from another long-claw, if he dared venture away from his claimed food area, but without physical confrontations. That wasn't necessary either. There was plenty for all. The supply was renewed daily.

Still, there was something lacking. It felt like he had a big hole in his heart. Although he had always been a solitary creature, he missed the other forest dwellers. He missed the stinging buzzers, the hissing quilled ones, the nodas, the kodas, the tovas. He was pleased to share the feeding ground with ringtails and squeakers. He enjoyed their presence. Nevertheless, Kuru chose to live with the hole in order to get the food, the food, the food, the unending, abundant food. Every single day food to his heart's content, except for the hole.

Once Kuru started back up the dirt trail toward the wide path that led past the uprights' nests. But when he reached the path, he was hungry, so he turned around and went back to the feeding ground. Another time he got as far as the uprights' big nest where he had communicated with a strong and commanding upright. Again he turned around. The lure of the feeding ground was too powerful.

* * *

It was the job of one of the workers at Baldwin Lake Lodge to load the garbage onto the flat bed pick-up truck after dinner and drive it to the dump site located about five miles from the camp. Every year, just before the opening of the lodge, large galvanized bins were set in place in the clearing to receive the summer's garbage. Every year the bears devastated the area. Every year it was cleared at the end of the summer season and the refuse flown out. This schedule coordinated well with the annual feeding-hibernation routine of the bears. When the lodge opened in the spring, the bears were awake from their winter sleep and ready to feed. In the early fall season they stopped their gorging and found a place to hibernate until spring.

John, an Oji-Cree, volunteered to be the sanitation worker this year. Not the favorite job of the employees. Mark was grateful that John had offered to take the position. He was behind the main lodge sharpening axes when John drove up. "How's it going out there, John?"

"The usual, boss. The bears are not neat eaters."

"That's for sure."

"But today I happened to notice one of the bears—one that feeds fairly close to the road—he had a real nasty scar on his muzzle, just below the left eye."

"Oh, yeah?"

"Didn't stop him from finding food, though!"

Mark laid aside the axe he was working on and went to find Meredith. She was still in the dining hall chatting with some late diners. He waited to catch her eye. He motioned for her to meet him in the office.

"What is it, Mark?"

"John just came back from the dump and guess what he saw."

"A lot of garbage and a bunch of bears. What?"

"A bear with a bad scar below the left eye."

"Our suspect in the mauling!"

"Looks like he's become a resident."

"We also have another suspect." She handed him a copy of the article she had printed out from the Chicago Tribune.

* * *

Kuru

The dark time had lengthened. The wind carried a chill that spoke of the white season. There was a restlessness in all the forest creatures. Kuru felt it. He had grown fat from the uprights' food offerings. He seemed to be searching for something. And something was urging him, beckoning him, taking control of him. His trips to the feeding ground were less frequent. He ate less than usual. He noticed there were fewer long-claws at their posts.

Finally it happened. He started out for the feeding ground at first light but instinct took him away from the food area and out onto the dirt trail that led to the wide path. When he stopped at the pond for a drink, he found the water much colder. He was careful not to step on a walking shell as he returned to the wide path. After a while he came to the uprights' big and little nests. The smell of their food had now become familiar to him. This time the aroma made him queasy. It was not food that he needed now. It was a place. He didn't know which place but he knew he was going to it.

And so Kuru began his return journey, the long journey home. At the edge of the rocky path he entered the shelter of the forest. He stopped, lifted his head to sniff the air. For the first time in a long while he could smell spruce and pine, long ears, bushy-tailed tree jumpers, even the scaley swimmers. He could hear the chickadees and the swish of poplar leaves in the wind. The urge to find the place grew more and more forceful and gave him strength to continue the arduous trek.

When the first dark time approached, he wandered along the water's edge, turned over some moss, and ate. He pulled up some greens and ate leaves and roots. Now he was ready to sleep. He chose a spot in a clump of grasses and lay down. Before he closed his eyes he sensed a change, something was different. Yes, something had changed. The hole in his heart was gone.

Chapter Ten
Kenora

Eric froze. A visitor? Is that what she said? He could think of only one thing: the police. A Canadian Mounty? The FBI? Whoever it was, he had no choice. He had to go downstairs and face the music. Even if it meant being hauled off to prison for the rest of his life. He abandoned hope, his heart fell to the bottom of his spirit, his shoulders slumped, as he locked his room and descended the stairs. He walked into the parlor ready to be handcuffed and treated like a criminal, not only a fugitive from justice, but in their eyes, a murderer.

A tall, athletic black man standing in front the fireplace turned to face him. Dressed in light gray slim pants and a form-fitting dark gray polo shirt, he projected pride in his healthy physique.

"Terrence? I'm Darius Hastings, the owner of the UTV and the little cabin." He stepped forward and held out a hand. Eric, speechless, shook his hand. "Sorry you found the cabin in such poor condition. I just purchased it this spring. Plan to fix it up real nice before the cold weather settles in. Did you have any problems with the vehicle? That's one heck of a ride to Kenora, isn't it? There should have been plenty of gas at the cabin."

"No, no problems and yes, there was plenty of gas." Eric was relieved that the man was not law enforcement but felt threatened that someone knew where he was. "How did you know where to find me?"

"I've never met your brother, but he has done an incredible job arranging things to protect you. A messenger delivered a hand-written note outlining the basics of my part of the plan. I was paid handsomely for the use of the cabin and UTV. I know really very little about what's going on, and I don't want to. Right now, I'm on my way back up to get started on the cabin spruce-up. The last thing I am to do is pick up the vehicle from you."

"So you don't know why I'm here, why all the hush-hush?"

"That's right. I just figure you're in some sort of serious legal trouble and that you're probably innocent."

"And you have no news from my brother about my daughter?"

"No, man. Like I said, I know next to nothing except what I'm supposed to do. And now I have extra money to fix up my cabin in time to do some hunting. I'm happy about that."

Eric walked over to the desk and took the UTV key off the pegboard. "Yes, it was quite a ride." He gave the key to Darius.

"Look, man. I truly hope things work out for you. And if you're into fishing or bear or moose hunting, I'll be renting my cabin out when I'm not using it. Get in touch." He handed Eric a business card.

Hastings Real Estate
1208 Washington Street
Saint Paul, MN 55107

Call Darius (651) 555-2400
I'll help you find a home or business location
in the greater Minneapolis-St Paul area

Eric slipped the card into a pants pocket. "Thank you, Darius. For everything. I know you took a risk to help me out. I could have wrecked your beautiful Massimo!"

"I did think about that, but, as I said, I was paid very nicely."

"It's in the garage behind the house. I'll take you to it."

Darius extended his hand again and walked to the front door. Eric led him to the garage and watched as Darius started up the engine then turned to him. "Good luck, Terrence. I hope I hear from you." He drove off, leaving Eric with the familiar smell of gasoline fumes.

Eric stood for a minute trying to process what just happened. Alan had certainly planned every little detail. He was glad that Darius knew nothing, but sorry that he had no news from home. At least he didn't have to worry with or about the UTV anymore. He closed the garage door and went back around the house. When he entered the hallway Margie called from the kitchen.

"Terrence, is that you? Did your friend leave? I was going to invite him to stay for dinner."

"He's gone. He just came to pick up his UTV. I had borrowed it. But that's truly kind of you." Eric went to the door of the kitchen. Margie, wearing a tailored white blouse and blue sailor pants, was at the stove stirring something in a pot. The aroma of fresh herbs filled the room. *She has such good taste in clothing ... and food.*

"Come on in and have a seat at the kitchen table. Dinner is informal tonight since there will be just the three of us."

"Oh? Another guest?"

"No. My daughter. She's back from her work as a counselor at a summer camp. Leaves for her first year of college in a week."

"She must be about seventeen?"

"Actually just sixteen. She skipped a grade in school." Margie went down the hall and knocked on a door at the back. "Josey, dinner's ready. Don't let it get cold." She returned to the kitchen and smiled at Eric.

"Go ahead and sit down, Mr. McElvin. Take the seat at the end." She poured two glasses of white wine, set them out for the adults, and began filling the plates at the stove. "I roasted a chicken. Do you prefer white meat or dark?"

"Dark ... or either really." Eric was glad the meal wasn't being served family style. He felt awkward passing bowls and things. She sat his plate on a floral placemat in front of him. Chicken leg and thigh with creamed potatoes and peas. It looked and smelled divine. She put two more filled plates on the table— hers and her daughter's—and sat down. "Josey will get here eventually. She has trouble tearing herself away from her cell phone. I think you said you had a daughter, if I'm not mistaken."

"I do. But she's only ten. No teen-age worries yet." Eric smiled to think of his girl becoming a teenager.

"Josey works with the eight-to-ten age girls at camp. She says they are mostly angelic! I hope that's true of your girl. What did you say her name is?"

Eric's blood ran cold. He didn't know how to answer. He had already mentioned Becca to Billy and Jake. Somehow it seemed safe then. But now, he didn't want to make a mistake. Charlie had said 'Everybody knows Margie.' "Uh, her name is Becky."

"Is that short for Rebecca?"

Thank God Josey came in at that moment. Tight jeans and two oversized tank tops.

"Josey, this is Mr. McElvin. He'll be having dinner with us for a while."

Josey slid into her seat. "Hi." Spoken with no inflection. She eyed her food, picked up a fork, and nibbled on some peas.

Eric took advantage of the turn of attention away from his daughter's name. "I hear you're off to college soon." He watched her dip into the potatoes.

"University of Manitoba, in Winnipeg. It's only about three hours away. Far enough but not too far, if you know what I mean."

"I'll keep that in mind when my daughter reaches the college stage."

"Mr. McElvin has a ten-year-old girl. I told him you worked with that age in camp," Margie interjected.

"How long will you be staying here?" Josey went for the chicken.

"Josey, that's not nice!"

"It's okay. I'm not sure right now. Probably a few weeks—as soon as my business gets settled."

"What kind of business are you in?" All teenage inhibitions gone.

"I'm an automotive mechanic. In fact, Margie, I meant to tell you I did take the job Charlie offered me on a trial basis."

"How wonderful! You can't go wrong working for Charlie."

"Mum, may I be excused?" Boring adult conversation no doubt.

"No dessert?"

"I'm good. Nice to meet you, Mr. McElvin. Good luck with your new job." Back to the electronics.

"She certainly is courteous."

"Margie grinned and shook her head. "Not always.""

Dessert was a scrumptious lemon tart. Then coffee. The two of them talked well past the dinner hour. Margie wanted to tell Eric, aka Terrence, everything about Kenora and its citizens. He rose from the table having learned that there were places he wanted to visit, things he would like to do in this little town on a big lake.

Lying awake in his room, Eric realized that he felt something he hadn't felt in a long time. He had enjoyed a moment of happiness this evening. His invented life was beginning to take over the real one. His new life was becoming more desirable than the old one. With one major exception. He missed Becca, her hearty laugh, her smiling eyes, her squeals when he teased her, her yawns during story time. He didn't want to miss out on all that. She would soon be a young lady like Josey. He didn't want to miss out on that either.

* * *

Eric hopped out of bed with new purpose. He was going to work today, he was going to be an auto mechanic again, eager to see what repair jobs Charlie had for him. He pulled on his thrift shop jeans—they were actually Levi's—and a tan T-shirt. His old navy-blue hoodie would keep away the chill until the temperature rose. Coffee and muffins were waiting in the kitchen as usual. Margie was probably grocery shopping, he guessed, and immediately wondered what she would prepare for dinner. It was something to look forward to all day.

The walk to the auto shop was brisk and refreshing. He passed the overgrown lawns and houses with peeling paint.

"Sorry, but I don't think I'll be doing that work for you." He reached the shop a little before eight. On the elevated Petro-Canada sign the red maple leaf emblem shone in the morning sun. The bays were open and the station was busy. He went into the main door and found Charlie talking to a customer.

"Hey, Terrence, be right with you." Eric entertained himself looking at fan belts, spark plugs, and other supplies for sale in the office. Charlie wore his gray jumpsuit with the name "Charlie" in an oval patch sewn on the left side. He ran the customer's credit card then walked over to Eric.

"Morning! Ready to go to work?"

"Ready and eager."

"The Ranchero is still in bay one. An F-150 and a Honda Civic are in the others. You can keep going on the Ranchero this morning. The owner wants it in top shape."

"I'm going to need some parts."

"Make me a list, leave it on my desk, and I'll take care of it."

"Will do."

Eric spent the morning going over the Ranchero with a fine-toothed comb. He felt good about working again and he felt especially good about getting an iconic classic car back in condition. He checked the interior for wear and tear. In the glove box he found a small leather case containing registration and insurance information. The car was registered to a Charles K. Abbott. He quickly zipped the case and closed the glove box.

"So the truck belongs to Charlie, not to a customer!" He sat on the passenger side of the front bench with an elbow on the center arm rest. "That explains a lot of things. He's the one who wants this car in top shape. Well, that's the way he's going to have it." He climbed out of the vehicle and went back to his job, checking everything from headlights to tailpipe. By noon he had the list complete.

"Here you go, boss. Not really that much to order. I did find a cracked exhaust manifold and a couple of interior knobs missing—in addition to the fuel line and filter I mentioned yesterday. And I'll replace plugs and belts."

"I'll get in on it this afternoon. Pull up that stool over there and let's eat. Nancy—that's my wife—fixed us both a lunch." He took two brown paper bags out of a lower desk drawer and tossed one to Eric. "Maybe you could get us a couple of drinks out of the machine." He slid a set of keys to Eric. "On the house."

As days went by Eric certainly was saving on food costs. A muffin and coffee at the rooming house, Nancy's bag lunches, and Margie's scrumptious dinners. He felt a little guilty accepting free food, but then again, he wanted to save the meager salary he earned each week. At the Canadian Tire Store he bought a strong box to house the cash and kept it out of sight in the closet. With all that seemed to be going well in Kenora, Eric had three oppressive worries: What was happening with the PI's search for the killer? What could Alan and Kathy tell Becca about the extended absence of her mother and father? Was the collision shop being well-managed without him or was he losing money? The worries abated when he was at work on the Ranchero and at dinner with Margie, bright moments in an otherwise anxiety-ridden and solitary existence.

Charlie became more talkative than usual one day at lunch.

"You say Margie is a great cook? I'm not surprised. That lady has always been special. You know she and I went to high school together. She was extremely popular, and smart. A real beauty, too. All the boys were in love with her!"

"She's still very nice-looking."

"I've never been inside her house, but I hear it looks like something out of a magazine."

"Yes, it does. And it's spotlessly clean."

"You tell Margie that old Charlie Abbott sends his regards."

"Sure."

That evening, after Josey had excused herself from the table, Eric mentioned his lunch-time conversation with Charlie.

"Oh, that Charlie! Drove a loud hotrod in those days. He has always been into cars." She took a bite of chocolate cake. "I'll confess something to you. In those days Charlie had a big crush on me. He kept asking me out and I kept finding excuses not to accept until finally I gave in and went to a school dance with him. He picked me up in a cream-colored 1947 Packard limousine! I was embarrassed to death! Classic cars were far from chic in my circles. Now of course I realize how beautiful and unique it was."

"Probably a Super Clipper. ' Forty-seven was the last year they made the long wheelbase for the limos. How did the date go?"

"At the dance he was all left feet, didn't offer to go for ice cream or anything afterwards, and was terribly awkward trying to give me a kiss goodnight, which I skillfully avoided. Now don't you dare repeat any of this to him! We are still on a friendly speaking basis."

"Your secret is safe with me, Ma'am."

"You know, Mr. McElvin, I can keep secrets, too."

"Margie, please call me Terry." Eric didn't know why he said that. His name wasn't even Terrence, much less it's diminutive. His relationship with Margie had ceased being formal and "Mr. McElvin" sounded even less like who he was.

"If ever you feel like sharing, I'm a good listener. I can recognize a burdened man."

"I appreciate that, Margie, but I just can't . . . for many reasons."

She reached over and briefly put her hand on his. "I understand."

"But I would like to ask you a question. How did you get paid for my room and half board here?"

"A messenger service brought me a money order in the full amount for a month's room and one meal a day. It came from an anonymous sender in Detroit, Michigan. Included was a type-written note with the date of your arrival. With all that, I knew someone was in trouble."

"You got that right." Eric stood up. "Thank you for another delicious meal. I'm going to get fat!" He took his dishes to the sink then turned around to her.

"Goodnight, Margie."

"Goodnight, Terry. Sleep well."

Eric walked slowly back up the stairs to his room. "I wish I could tell Margie what's going on. It would give me some relief just to relate the whole business to someone. And she's such a fine person. I'm sure I could trust her. *Don't tell anyone anything.* When all this is over and they find the killer, I will tell her the whole story." Alone in the room, he stretched across the bed feeling fatigued, not because of his job, but because of the strain of maintaining a false persona. How he wanted to say to Margie and to Charlie, "My name is Eric Sanders. I live in Chicago where I run a collision shop. I have a fantastic daughter and the world's best brother to whom I owe my life. You wouldn't believe the journey I had from Cinnamon Lake in Manitoba to Kenora." More than anything he wanted to talk to Becca. He imagined what he would say to her if he could call her. "Kitten, you know I'm innocent. I would never do anything to hurt your mother. I miss you both so much. When I get back home, I'm going to take you to Canada and teach you how to catch big fish. You'll see all sorts of wildlife—even moose and bears! And you will like my friends Margie and Charlie."

Eric fell asleep fully clothed.

Chapter Eleven
Murder

One month before the bear attack

Sam Clark sat in his brand-new burgundy Nissan Altima. He had just bought it with the money from his first job. That hit had been easy. No loose ends, no messy screw-ups, no close calls. Just fast, easy money. Not that he particularly liked the work, but a man's gotta do what a man's gotta do. And he was going to get good at it. He took a deep whiff of that oh-so-delightful new car smell, pulled out the pint from under the front seat, unscrewed the cap, and drank. *Just a sip or two to take the edge off.* He had promised himself that he would not touch any alcohol on the job. Afterwards, yes. Plenty afterwards. But this neighborhood was really nice. Not super rich, but comfortable. Typical successful middle-class America. Not the trailer parks and cheap apartments he expected to be dealing with.

"I could live here. A wife, kids, a van ...." He took another sip. "Nah, that's not for me." He replaced the cap and returned the bottle to its place.

Outdoor lights popped on. A man came out of the house, got into a van, and backed down the driveway. Sam noticed the writing painted on the side. *Sanders Auto Repair and Collision Shop.* "Bet that's the boyfriend now. Women. Cheating bitches. I oughta take him out, too." A woman stood at the open door watching the man drive off, her arm around the shoulders of a little girl. "Funny nobody mentioned a kid. That could complicate things."

He waited, watching the house lights, hoping the outside lights were motion activated and would go out any minute or the woman would turn them off from inside. She did. There were a few lights on in the house. "C'mon, bitch, tuck the girl in and go to bed." Sam checked his weapon. Full clip. He slipped on the new latex gloves. A good fit. Not too tight for his trigger finger, but tight enough to give him agility. He had memorized the address: 431 Oak Park Drive and verified with the street sign and the number on the mailbox. And here he was, waiting. The waiting was the hardest part for Sam. Tension builds up, nerves get sensitive, doubts creep in. Finally all was quiet and dark except for one dim light. "Night light for the girl or reading lamp for the girlfriend." Sam eased open the car door and closed it with hardly a sound. He approached the house from the side. Sticking close to the tall bushes, he spotted the back door. "Opens into the kitchen." Sam was given a detailed description of the interior. "Straight down the hall. Bedroom on left."

The simple lock was easily dispatched. But the back door opened into a laundry room, not the kitchen. "Something's wrong here." Beyond the washer and dryer Sam could see that the dim light was on in the adjoining room. With his back to the wall, he peered around. The woman, fully clothed and wearing an apron, stood at a steel sink in the kitchen. Sam glanced around the kitchen taking in every detail, just in case. Kid's drawing of an elephant on the refrigerator door, orange and white tablecloth, an unused place setting, a few dishes left to be rinsed, apron printed with little Eiffel Towers. Sam stepped into the doorway, released the safety.

"Eric is that you?" Before he could aim, the woman turned and screamed. Everything went into fast forward. She had a knife, came toward him, he pushed her away but the knife caught his right shoulder, his hand released the gun. He heard it thud to the hardwood floor. The woman was down but her fingers still held the knife.

Sam threw himself on top of her. She twisted, kicked, and struggled. She was not easily subdued, but Sam managed to overpower her, pull the knife from her clutch and stab her several times in the chest. The squirming stopped. She lay still. It took Sam a minute to realize what had just happened. Blood began to engulf the Eiffel towers. She was not moving. Sam could not detect the in-and-out of her breathing. He knelt to feel her throat for a pulse. Nothing. The woman was dead. His job was done. Not the way it was supposed to go, but it was over. *Better get the heck out of here.* He put the knife down on the counter, picked up the gun and pocketed it. The girl! He had forgotten about the girl. Did she see anything, hear anything? Check on the kid, then *go*.

"Mama? Are you in the kitchen?"

My God, she's up and headed for the kitchen. Rather than face the necessity of having to harm a child, Sam fled through the laundry room and out the way he came in. Around the house, past the tall bushes, he reached his car, hit the Nissan start button, and left the scene as quickly but as quietly as possible.

"Keep the speed down." Sam didn't want to attract the attention of any neighborhood patrol car. Heart running fast, adrenalin pumping, hard to drive slowly. The route to his apartment seemed endless. He was relieved to join a main thoroughfare with brightly-lit twenty-four-hour pharmacies and grocery stores. When he finally wheeled into the parking lot of his apartment building he pulled into the nearest available slot and cut the motor. He leaned back against his seat, took a few deep breaths. He had never used a knife as a weapon before. The bloody latex gloves were still on his hands. Blood was smeared on the steering wheel of his new car.

"Jeez, I've gotta clean that up!" He stripped off the gloves turning them inside out. "And get rid of these." He stashed them in the jacket pocket that held the gun. Taking a cloth from the glove box he wiped the steering wheel with the meticulous care of a surgeon cleaning a wound.

He exited the vehicle, discarded the cloth and gloves in the building's large waste bin and headed for the main door. Once inside his apartment he poured himself a sizeable glass of bourbon and collapsed on the couch. His hands were shaking. Liquor spilled out onto his shirt. He tried to piece together what had happened. The more he thought about it the more he didn't want to think about it. Another bourbon, and another until he couldn't think about it or anything else for that matter. His head fell back, his eyes closed, and the memory of the night's work was temporarily erased.

"Only my second job. Hope I didn't screw it up too bad" was his last thought before being lost to the world for several hours.

* * *

With her cut finger wrapped in Eric's shirt, Sandy thought it would be a good time to convince him to stay home tonight. Yet she felt guilty for asking. "Mainly for Rebecca. She's devoted to you, Honey, and wants to spend more time with you, share things with you. Like tonight. Her favorite Disney movie is on television and she wants you to see it, watch it with her. Can't you finish that repair job tomorrow?"

"Wish I could. But, look, I promise you and Becca that I'll be here every night the rest of the week. I have to do the work tonight. The owner is coming in from out of state to pick up the car tomorrow. There, now. You've stopped bleeding." He unwrapped and released her hand. "Better go bandage it up."

She knew there was no way to persuade him. If he wouldn't do it for Rebecca, he just wouldn't do it. Period. He gave them both a hug and kiss, picked up his keys from their place on the hall table near the front door. Sandy and Becca followed.

"'Night, girls."

"Night, Dad."

"I'll wait up for you, Honey."

They watched him back down the driveway. Sandy noticed a car parked in front of her neighbor's house. "I wonder who could be visiting the Carlsens? I've never seen that car before." She stood for a moment before turning off the outside light. "Maybe I should leave it on for Eric. No, I'll be up." She found some Band-Aids in the bathroom cabinet, chose a large one, and wrapped it around the wounded finger awkwardly with one hand. Rebecca had already run to the TV and was engrossed in animation when Sandy slipped in beside her on the couch. By the end of the movie

Becca was asleep with her head on the arm of the couch, cartoon figures swirling in and out of dreams.

"Rebecca, wake up, Sweetie. Time for bed." The drowsy ten-year-old made no resistance. Within minutes pajamas were on, teeth brushed, covers tucked, Buddy Bear in arms, eyes closed. Sandy was tired and sleepy, too. Long day at Macy's. Rush home to prepare dinner. She and her daughter enjoyed the chicken casserole. Her husband would eat late. Probably ten or ten thirty. But she would wait up and the two of them would tell each other about their day while he had dinner. Just the two of them sharing. Like it once was. A chance to start closing up the void that had formed between them.

She turned off the bedroom light but left Rebecca's door partially open. Back in the kitchen she tied her apron on again and started the clean-up. Under the soft light above the sink she rinsed flatware and glasses and put them in the dishwasher. The process of loading was taking longer than usual since it was a one-handed job. She didn't want to wet the bandage on her left index finger. She picked up a plate to rinse and heard a click. She sensed someone in the house.

"Eric is that you?" She turned. A man stood in the kitchen door. It was not Eric. She saw the gun. "No-o-o!" she screamed. In a nano-second her hand found the slicing knife that was lying on the counter. The same knife Eric had taken from her when he wrapped her bleeding hand in his shirttail.

* * *

Eric looked at the round black-and-white clock on the shop wall. "This is taking longer than I thought." Another half hour passed before he washed up at the sink in the back, scrubbed hands and forearms well with Working Hands. He used a stiff nail brush, refusing to be a mechanic with black under and around his nails. He dried off, closed and locked up the shop. Eager to get home, eat, and get to bed, he hoped Sandy would wait up for him like she had said. "We've sure drifted apart. It's just not like it used to be. And it's my fault. I know it is. Too many hours at the shop. Too many birthdays and anniversaries not celebrated. Not enough attention paid to the family. Got to change that."

Eric pulled the van up in the driveway and hurried to the front door. He was determined to fix his marital relationship the same way he fixed cars. The same dedication, the same patience, the same intensity. He plopped his keys in the decorative basket on the hall table.

"Sandy girl, are you awake?" Hey, Babe, did you wait up?"

He looked down the hall. Becca's door was ajar, the master bedroom open and dark.

"She's already in bed asleep." He went into the kitchen for his regular glass of bedside water and found his wife on the floor bleeding.

"Oh, my God! Oh, my God! Sandy!" He flew to the body and saw the blood soaking the apron and spilling onto the hardwood. He knelt and slid an arm under her shoulders.

"Sandy, can you hear me? Honey, answer me." Even in a state of shock, he realized his wife was dead. Murdered. "This is not happening. Call 911. No. First call Alan to come."

Alan and Kathy lived in an upscale neighborhood twenty minutes away. Twenty long, dreadful minutes. Eric walked around the kitchen, returning to his wife's body until he couldn't look at her anymore. In twenty minutes Alan and Kathy arrived. A few minutes later one police squad car, an unmarked car, an ambulance, and a firetruck pulled up in front of the Sanders' house.

* * *

"Tell us what happened, Mr. Sanders." The detective took a notepad and pen out of his coat pocket, flip it open, and prepared to write.

"I don't know. When I came in from work I found my wife . . . like that." Eric sat on the sofa, Alan beside him. Kathy had found Rebecca asleep in her room and had whisked her out the front, into the car, and was on the way home before the responders arrived.

"What time was that?"

"Around eleven o'clock I think."

"Do you always work that late?"

"Once or twice a week."

"Did you two have any marital problems?"

"No. She didn't like me working late but accepted it okay."

"Can you think of anyone who would want to harm her? Anyone at her job?"

"No one. Absolutely no one." Eric lowered his head and put his hands over his face.

"Everybody loved Sandy. She was a good, sweet person." Alan interjected. "Can we do this later?"

"Your brother will need to come to the station to make an official statement and, if he agrees, take a polygraph."

"I'll bring him in first thing tomorrow."

"Bring the daughter in, too."

"Is that absolutely necessary? She knows nothing."

"Let us determine that."

"Just one more thing, Mr. Sanders. Is that blood on your shirt?"

"My wife cut her finger and I wrapped it and applied pressure to stop the bleeding."

"You need to let me take that shirt for the lab to test. Just routine."

Eric obliged. "It's got a lot of grease and dirt on it, too. I was going to put it in the laundry basket before bed."

"Don't worry about that." An officer handed the detective a plastic evidence bag.

Alan took off his hoodie and gave it to Eric. When the siblings reached the front door they had to duck under yellow crime scene tape. The forensic unit was already at work.

* * *

The night at Alan's crept by. Eric wrestled with demons of guilt, anger, and inconsolable grief. Overriding all were the questions "Who?" and "Why?" He hadn't even seen his daughter much less spoken with her. Did she see or hear anything? What if she witnessed the attack? In a way he hoped she had. If so, it would help the police find the killer. But then again he hoped she hadn't been exposed to the brutality of a stabbing at her young age. Not just a stabbing, but the stabbing of her mother. If she knew nothing, he would make sure the police handled her questioning without revealing Sandy's death. He would do his best to shield her from the pain as long as he could.

The thought of going back to the house tortured him. How could he walk into the kitchen again? How could he go through Sandy's belongings? How could he bear to look at a photo of her without disintegrating? No, he had to stay strong for Becca. She was solely his responsibility now. A motherless child. The reality of those words flooded him with overwhelming despair, he lost control, and wept.

Alan woke him at seven. "Kathy has set out a little breakfast for all of us. I would like to get you and Rebecca to the station by eight. Do you think you can eat something?"

"I'm not hungry, but Becca needs to eat."

"At least have a cup of coffee."

"Do you think she saw what happened? Has she mentioned it?"

"Kathy doesn't think she knows anything or saw anything. She's just confused about having to come to her aunt's and uncle's house to sleep."

"I really wish the police didn't need to question her. They might tell her about the assault and even the murder." The word felt foreign to him, especially in connection to a member of his family, someone he loved. Alan, I don't want her to know yet."

"I understand. Now, go ahead. Get dressed. There's a clean shirt for you on the dresser. I'll meet you downstairs."

Rebecca was at the table finishing a bowl of Frosted Flakes. Kathy had enough presence of mind to bring along an outfit for the girl: deep pink calf-length cotton pants and a crisp white tailored blouse. As soon as she saw him, she ran up and threw her arms around his waist.

"Daddy, what's going on?" she asked in earnest.

"Oh, some man broke into the house last night but he didn't steal anything, The police are after him. Nothing to worry about, Sweetie. But they do need to ask you some questions this morning. Are you okay with that?"

"Um-hum. But where is Mom?"

"I'll tell you later. Right now we need to go."

Alan handed him a styrofoam cup of hot black coffee and the two men, Kathy, and Rebecca proceeded to the couple's Mercedes sedan.

"Don't spill it on the upholstery. I just had it replaced at Sanders Auto Repair and Collision Shop."

"I'll be super careful. I'm sure they charged you an arm and a leg." The camaraderie Eric had with his brother gave him the courage he so needed now.

* * *

"Hello, Little Lady. Rebecca. Right?" Becca nodded. "My name is Detective Trexler. Thank you, Rebecca, for agreeing to talk with me. I need to ask you about last night. Did your mother put you to bed?"

"Um-hum."

"Do you remember what time that was?"

"After the movie."

"So that would be about ten?"

"I think so."

"Now after your mother left your room, did you see or hear anything unusual?"

Rebecca looked down at her feet.

"You can tell me. It's okay."

"I heard Mom yell and scream."

"And did you get out of bed?"

"I wanted to find out why she yelled. I thought maybe a mouse."

"What else did you see or hear?"

"I heard funny noises in the kitchen, so I went to see."

"And what did you see, Rebecca?"

"I saw a man run into the laundry room. I got scared and went back to my room."

"Can you tell me what the man looked like?"

She looked down again.

"Go ahead. You're doing great."

"I just saw the back of him for just a minute. He was gone. Fast."

"You didn't see his face? Could the man have been your Daddy going back out to his van to get something?"

"Maybe. I don't think so. I think it was a repair man."

"What did you do then in your room?"

"I got back in bed and went to sleep but Aunt Kathy woke me up and took me to her house."

"Thank you for telling me all this. You've been extremely helpful."

* * *

As soon as the police cleared the crime scene, Eric was allowed back in the house. It pained him to be in the place where his wife was murdered, but he endured it. Rebecca stayed with Alan and Kathy. He wanted to put the house on the market. However, he knew agents would be hesitant to show the "Murder House," and Eric could not bring himself to do the needed repairs or arrange for upgrades. He spent most of his time at the shop or at Alan's. The police interviewed Eric's and Sandy's colleagues at work. They called Alan, Kathy, and Rebecca back in for questioning. Nothing led anywhere. One of Sandy's coworkers claimed that Sandy told her she and Eric were not close anymore. She was afraid he might ask for a divorce. Investigators discovered a $200,000 insurance policy on Sandra Sanders taken out by her husband. No one could verify the husband's alibi. So Eric remained the prime and only suspect.

Alan was tormented, in fear of a wrong outcome to this investigation. A tragedy. He couldn't sleep, constantly thinking about a solution, some way to prove Eric's innocence. But not a thing came to mind. But maybe he could buy some time.

"Kat, they're gonna arrest him I'm sure. I have to do something. I can't just standby and see my brother accused of murder and hauled off to prison, possibly death row."

There in the darkness, with Kathy nestled beside him listening, he put together a plan to save his brother.

"It can be done. It won't be easy, but it can be done."

Chapter Twelve
At the Lodge

Hi Meredith and Mark,

It's me Billy, your troublesome customer. You guys were so good to come to the hospital to see me. I'm sorry I wasn't able to be more cooperative. It took me a few days to get my bearings (no pun intended). My wife spoke to you in the hospital cafeteria. She said you were very kind and generous to refund our deposit and pay for our flights. That was more than generous. I am writing to tell you that I received the article and photo you sent of the man who disappeared from his home in Chicago. At first glance I said "Yes, that's Terrence all right." But on close inspection I'm not so sure. Terrence did not have hair that dark and something about the eyes is not quite the same. The main thing is Terrence just didn't seem like a guy who would commit murder, much less murder his wife. If I recall, he did speak fondly of his wife during our week at Cinnamon Lake but I don't think he mentioned her name. Anyway, I thought you might like to know that I called the CPD and explained about the bear attack and our fishing partner who went missing. They said they would look into it. So if you get a call from the Chicago police, you'll know what it concerns.

Thanks again and see you next year!!
Billy Stiles

P.S. Let me know if you locate Terrence.

Meredith sat blinking and thinking. "What have I done? Have I opened a can of worms? What if poor Terrence really is dead, a second and fatal victim of the bear? The police will surprise his family with the news that he is a murder suspect. Of course, if they find that his wife is alive, I guess they'll know he's not their man." Meredith pulled up the Chicago Tribune and began searching and reading. "Maybe there are some new developments in the case." She hadn't been reading long when her computer alerted her to a new email.

Hey Mark and Meredith,

I printed out a copy of the photo you sent of the man who is missing from his home in Chicago and have been studying it. It sure looks a lot like Terrence but I just can't identify him positively. I do remember that at the lake he said he enjoyed cooking (He was our chef!) but rarely got a chance because he worked late a lot so his wife always prepared the meals. Have you thought about contacting the Chicago police? I could do it, except I don't want to get anybody in trouble.

Thanks for finding us a date in June for next summer. So far just me and Billy, but I'm sure we'll pick up another fisherman or two before then. I've already ordered four cans of bear spray!!

Jake Barnes

Meredith pressed "Reply."

Hi Jake,

Wanted to let you know that I also heard from Billy about the photo. He wasn't absolutely sure either. He saw a resemblance but really couldn't say. But he has contacted the Chicago police. They might call me for details. I'll let you know what happens. Like you, I don't want to cause trouble for anyone.

Your cabin is reserved for you next June 21-29. Remember we fly you in and out on Sunday.

So glad you guys decided to renew. Let me know if you hear or read anything about the murder suspect.

Wishing you fair skies and hungry fish,

Meredith Marsten

Baldwin Lake Lodge

She barely had time to click on *Send* when someone rushed into the office.

"Jenny! Where have you been all summer? I've missed you!" She swiveled around to enjoy a hug from an excited little sister.

"I've missed you, too!" Keeping her arms around Meredith's neck she leaned back. "Tell me about the bear! Did it really hurt someone? One of our regulars?"

"No. A new guest. But he's okay now. But you haven't told me where you've been."

"I was at soccer camp in Red River. I made a lot of new friends and had a lot of fun."

"You already have *beaucoup de copains.*"

"Oui, tu as raison. But Mama said the bear came here to our lodge."

"A bear. Maybe or maybe not the same bear. We don't know."

"I guess they all do look sorta alike."

During the conversation with her sister Meredith could see from the office window that something was going on at the dock. A group of guests and guides pulled a man out of a boat and were helping him up the hill toward a cabin. He was not walking on his own.

What in the world has happened to him?

"Stay here, Peanut, I'll be back in a minute." Meredith left by the back door and sprinted toward the cabin. Mark and one of the guides got him on a bed and were taking off his boots.

"Mark, what happened?"

"There was a boating accident."

"How? Where?"

Mark pulled her aside. "Two boats collided and Mr. Cranston was knocked into the water. He evidently hit his head on the gunwhale and blacked out. The guide jumped in and kept him from drowning. They got him back in the boat but we don't know how badly he's hurt. They had spotted a bear on the shore and thought it was the Cinnamon Lake bear. Mr. Cranston was standing up using binoculars."

"I think the whole world is looking for that bear! How did it happen?"

"The wind was tricky, the boats were separated by a small peninsula. Both were trying to get a closer look at the bear and neither guide saw the other in time. There's no one to blame, except the bear for being in full view."

"That bear again! Will there be no end to the grief it's causing us? Jenny just arrived from soccer camp asking a million questions about the bear."

"The one they saw today couldn't be the same bear. This one was rust colored. The one at Cinnamon was standard black. But I do believe the scar-faced one that wandered into our camp a couple of weeks ago was the attack bear."

The injured Mr. Cranston was sitting on the side of the bed now.

"Mark, I think I'm okay. Just a little dizzy and there's a lump on my head. But I don't need a rescue helicopter. Your guide Jared here saved my life."

"Please, if you start to feel bad or have any problems at all, we will get you to a hospital."

"Really no need. I'll be back out fishing tomorrow. 'Till then I'll just rest here in the cabin."

"We'll keep checking on you. Someone will bring you your evening meal. Anything else you need just let us know."

Meredith and Mark walked back to the lodge together leaving Mr. Cranston with the three other members of his fishing party. The two guides went back to secure their boats.

Anxiety and frustration weighed heavily on Meredith. *What are we doing wrong? I've got to talk to Bobby and get his opinion and advice. He ran this lodge so flawlessly even before he married Mama. I just can't take any more bear trouble.*

When they reached the lodge Mark fell into his desk chair, put his head in his hands. He looked up at his wife. "Next week, the last week of camp, two guys and a guide have booked the Cinnamon Lake camp for a bear hunt. I'm not sure whether they are using rifles, shotguns, or bows, but I think they will have a good chance getting scarface for us."

"I'll pray to God, you ask the Great Spirit to help us out. I have never before wanted an animal to die, but I do now and hate that I feel that way."

"Same here. Let's just try to wait it out. One way or another, all this will end."

Meredith resumed her reading of the Tribune which was still up on the computer when the office phone rang.

"Baldwin Lake Lodge. This is Meredith Marsten. How can I help you?"

"Ms. Marsten, I'm Lieutenant Trexler with the Chicago Police Department. I understand you have a missing fisherman?"

"Last month we had a bear assault on a group of three guests at one of our outposts. One was flown to the hospital in Winnipeg, another was located without injury, but a third disappeared. We fear he may be a second and fatal victim of the bear."

"Do you mind if I ask you a few questions about this third and possible victim? We heard from a Billy Stiles that he resembled the picture of a man whose wife was murdered and who has since gone missing."

"Yes. Billy emailed me to that effect."

"Can you give me any information about the man?"

"His name is Terrence McElvin and he is from the Chicago area."

"Do you have an address or phone number for him?"

"No, I'm sorry. Billy was the contact person for the group. I imagine he has some way of reaching Terrence."

"He gave us an address—a post office box registered to a deceased person—and a cell number that turned out to be a burner phone. So no help there. Can you describe him for me? Any distinguishing features?"

"I never got a good look at him. He flew in from Winnipeg with all the other guests then boarded the float plane to get to the outpost. I was the pilot but still didn't get a chance to check him out. The three of them wore hoodies and began taking their gear into the cabin as soon as they deplaned. You have to realize that we have between twenty-five and thirty guests each week."

"I understand. Do you happen to know his wife's name?"

"No, I don't have any idea. I'm sorry we couldn't provide more information."

"One other thing, Ms. Marsten. I looked at a satellite map and spotted what looked like a clearing near Wheeler Lake. We think possibly he was picked up by helicopter there and flown to Winnipeg. We're working with the Mounties on that angle. Do you know if it's possible?"

"I suppose it's possible. I don't really know."

"Anyway, thank you for your time, Ms. Marsten. And if you locate the missing person, even if it's the body of a bear victim, please let us know right away and send us a photo. Meanwhile we'll continue to investigate this Terrence McElvin here in Chicago."

Trexler gave her his number. Meredith jotted the number down and hung up.

Would they really want a picture of a fatal bear mauling?

Meredith went back to the *Tribune*. The phone rang again.

"Baldwin Lake Lodge. This is Meredith Marsten. How can I help you?"

"Meredith, this is Jake. I just remembered that Terrence did say the name of his wife once up at the cabin. He called her Sandy. And I think I told you his daughter's name is Becky or Becca. Thought you'd like to know this before the police called."

"Hi, Jake. I just got off the phone with the Chicago Police Department. They specifically asked me if I knew his wife's name. Would you do me the favor of phoning them with this new information? They may even call you and Billy in for questioning. I have the number here. Ask for Lieutenant Trexler." Meredith repeated the number Trexler gave her.

"Will do. Sorry my timing wasn't any better. Have you found the big bad bear yet?"

"Not yet but we will. Take care, Jake."

"You, too."

Something rang a bell in Meredith's memory. She fished around in the papers scattered on Mark's desk and found the xeroxed Tribune article and reread it.

"The murdered wife's name is Sandra Sanders. Sandra. Sandy. Terrence McElvin is no doubt Eric Sanders!"

* * *

Meredith found Bobby in front of his cabin stacking wood. With his red and black flannel shirt and well-worn jeans, his dark curls streaked with gray, he looked like a skinny lumberjack.

"Hi, Mer. Come to chop some wood for me?"

"Yeah, and fell a few trees, too." She waited until he finished the pile.

"I need to talk to you, Bobby."

"What's up?"

"Um … It's this bear business." Her voice quivered. "It's gotten to me."

Bobby dusted off his hands and put an arm around her shoulders. "No. Not my fearless wilderness girl. Don't cave in, that's just not you."

"But it never seems to end. Did you hear about the boat accident?"

"I did, but it's not bad. Could have been a lot worse. The guy is okay. Same for the bear attack. Billy survived, healed and is coming back next year."

"It's all Jenny can talk about. And everybody keeps asking me if we have destroyed the bear or if we've found the missing man." They started walking over to the lodge, Bobby's arm still around her shoulders.

"Speaking of the missing man, Bobby, I think he is a killer."

"A killer?"

"I mean a suspect in a murder case. I think he may have killed his wife."

"What in the world are you talking about?"

Meredith recounted everything to Bobby—the *Tribune* article, the email exchanges, the conversation with Lieutenant Trexler, and her logical conclusion."

They had reached the back stoop of the lodge. Bobby turned to her, put both hands on her upper arms. "I know we sort of formed our own private investigator association, but our job was only to try to find our missing guest, not to get involved in police work. And we did all we could. It's totally in the hands of the Canadian and American authorities. Let them do their job."

Meredith lowered her head. "I don't think Mark and I are doing our job very well. All those years you and Mama ran the lodge, everything went smoothly. You never had bad things happen."

"Sit down here a minute." He motioned toward the steps to the stoop. "We certainly did have our problems. We tried to shield our worries from you. For example, there was a guy who couldn't get along with his guide. He was so verbally abusive that the guide refused to take him out any more, and likewise the guy refused to go with that guide. We had a full house with no guides to spare, so I had to be his guide for the rest of the week. Believe me, this guy was intolerable. And one year a group met for shore lunch. After the guide had prepared and set their food out on the picnic table, a mean-looking bear came into the shore spot. The group ended up sitting in the boats and watching the bear devour their lunch. I'm sure you remember the year that rainstorms ruined our hard landing strip and we had to scurry around and find helicopters to fly everyone in. You see, we had our nail-biting moments. But we got through each one just like you and Mark are doing."

"I do remember the helicopter year." Meredith reached over and kissed her stepfather on the cheek. "Thank you. But you forgot the time a regular guest Fed-Exed his rods, reels and tackle ahead of time but they never arrived. I remember Mama going around to all the fishermen asking them to donate some of their equipment. With her gentle persuasion the guy ended up with more and better gear than what he had sent."

"There you go. Listen, tomorrow, if the weather cooperates, you and I are going to take a break. I've got a secret fishing spot away from it all. We'll take a picnic lunch with ham sandwiches and have a little getaway. Meet me at the dock after the guests go out in the morning. Now I think I hear the crowd heading this way. Appetizers await us."

"We have a date!"

* * *

Chicago

Billy still couldn't lean back in a hard chair, so he sat bolt upright in front of the detective.

"Mr. Stiles, tell me how you hooked up with Terrence McElvin for this fishing trip a few weeks ago." Trexler sat across the table with a pencil behind his ear, a note pad in front of him. The collar of his light blue shirt was open and his dark blue tie had been loosened.

"Jake and I let it be known at a couple of taverns that we had reserved a fishing cabin in Canada and that there was room for up to four more people. The word got around, I guess."

"And this cabin was booked through a lodge?"

"Yessir. Baldwin Lake Lodge in Manitoba. About an hour's flight from Winnipeg."

"Did you know Terrence before this trip?"

"No, he called me out of the blue and arranged to meet me and Jake at O'Hare."

"How did he get your number?"

"He said some guy told him about it at a bar and gave him my number."

"And what was this Some Guy's name?"

"He never said."

"So you go trapsing off to a remote cabin in Canada with this man you didn't know anything about, no valid address, no valid phone number."

"It was a last-minute thing. I figured I'd scope him out at the airport. He scoped out fine. He paid for his part up front—in cash. And he was a good companion at the lake." Billy was getting annoyed with the way Trexler was wording things. *The detective is making it seem like he thinks I'm complicit in this murder or aiding and abetting a felon. I volunteered to come in for questioning. And it wasn't easy with this walking cane and my throbbing back. He owes me a little respect.*

"Was the third member of your party—this Mr. . . . ." Trexler consulted his notes ". . . Jake Barnes involved in the decision to take on McElvin?"

"Not at all. He left it all up to me."

"What do you think happened to McElvin after the bear attack?"

"I have no idea. He may have been eaten by the bear or else gotten lost in the wilderness and starved to death. The Canadian authorities put out a search party for several days and questioned lots of people. Perhaps you should talk to them. Or fly up to Baldwin Lake yourself. I've told you all I know. So if I'm free to go ...."

"Thank you, Mr. Stiles. We will contact you if we have further questions. And for the time being, please do not leave the state or the country."

Billy was a little miffed as he limped to the 'L' station. He would have to make one transfer and still take a cab to get home. He decided to call Uber.

"They should drive me home or pay my way. They're starting to think Terrence McElvin is Eric Sanders. But they'll never find him. I doubt that anyone will ever find him. Except maybe Meredith Marsten."

Chapter Thirteen
Kenora

Sandy had been appearing in Eric's dreams. Night after night vivid images of her troubled his sleep. He could see her but she couldn't see him. It was though he were the invisible man watching her going about her daily routine, her clothing drenched in blood. Then he would be at Darius' cabin but the UTV was missing. "I can't come for you, Sweetheart. There's no way I can get to you." He cowered inside the cabin where he could hear a vicious bear mauling people outside. He would wake up roiling and churning like an angry ocean. His chest hurt so bad he thought he might be having a heart attack.

One morning after a particularly disturbing night he sat up panting, heart pumping, sweating. He found it hard to get himself dressed and ready for work. He managed to make it downstairs to the coffee pot. In fact, he arrived early.

"Terry, what's wrong?" Margie had just taken fresh orange muffins out of the oven.

You look like you've seen a ghost."

"I have . . . I mean, I've been having rough nights, bad dreams."

"Do you feel okay, physically?"

"Not really. Some chest pain and perspiration." Eric took a few sips of hot coffee, sat at the table, his head propped on his hands.

Margie slipped off her polka dot oven gloves and sat down across from Eric. "Maybe you should see a doctor."

"I'll be okay, Margie. Don't worry about me. I always bounce back."

"It may not be my place to say, but I think you need a break from working so much. You work with Charlie all week then go in to work in the garage alone on weekends. In the evenings you just sit in your room watching television. Why don't you take a short weekend vacation? A little diversion is good medicine. There's a quote I like from the Desiderata: *Many fears are born of fatigue and loneliness.*" She reached over and put her hand on his arm, patted it as though he were a relative or close friend.

Eric raised his head and realized he was looking at a beautiful woman. Middle aged, but still young looking. She was no longer a bikini beach queen, but she carried her maturity well. Her grayish-green eyes radiated a *joie-de-vivre* tempered with the wisdom of living and enduring. Eric sensed her genuine compassion and felt grateful for that.

Eric smiled. "I vaguely remember the Desiderata."

"If you don't mind, I have a suggestion. You told me that you got a glimpse of the *Kenora* in the harbor and thought about taking one of her cruises. Why don't you do just that? Tomorrow is Saturday. You don't have to go to Charlie's. Go out on the lake instead, while the weather is still warm enough."

He thought about that idea for a moment. "Will you come with me? Uh . . . that is, if you don't have other commitments. Perhaps Josey would like to join us. See, I'm cooperating. I'm trying to do something about the 'fatigue and loneliness.'"

"I can arrange to be free tomorrow, Terry. I'll check with Josey but I doubt she will forego her live companions and electronic friends. Now let's get another cup of coffee and eat a muffin." She sat a still-steaming golden muffin flecked with orange peel in front of him. Eric inhaled.

"It smells divine." He took a bite. "Margie, this is the best thing I have ever put in my mouth!"

Margie smiled and picked up her cell phone. "I'm calling to set up a cruise for us tomorrow. I have the *Kenora* on speed dial since guests often ask me to make reservations for them. Will two o'clock be good?"

The cruise was a real treat for Eric. The big lake was not a smooth pond, but the *Kenora* rode the waves with dignity. The captain pointed out island after island, some with gorgeous homes, others with quaint log cabins and told stories about many of them. When he sailed by the Eagle Rock Lodge island enclave, Margie leaned close to speak above the engine noise. "You should have dinner there. It's a short boat ride from Kenora. They serve cocktails in the garden and a splendid meal in the lodge." For the remainder of the cruise Eric debated with himself whether he should invite Margie for a drink afterwards but finally decided against it.

The next few evenings a new guest took dinner at Margie's, so heart-to-heart talks with her had to be suspended. During that time Eric had a chance to think of ways to deal with his isolation. He thought about Margie's quote from the Desiderata. He remembered his mother had put a beautiful calligraphy version of it on the refrigerator door. He left Charlie's early one day, located an internet café, sat at one of the computer stations, pulled up the poem, and read through it several times. One section seemed to speak directly to him:

> *Nurture strength of spirit to shield you in sudden misfortune*
> *But do not distress yourself with dark imaginings*
> *Many fears are born of fatigue and loneliness*
> *Beyond a wholesome discipline*
> *be gentle with yourself*
> *You are a child of the universe*
> *no less than the trees and the stars*
> *you have a right to be here*
> *And whether or not it is clear to you*
> *No doubt the universe is unfolding as it should.*

As he read, scenes from his incredible journey through the Canadian wilderness flooded his brain. Visions of white pines and poplars, lakes with beavers, ducks, geese, and loons presented themselves one by one. He could smell the pine, hear quaking, clucking, and trills, the splat of a tail hitting the water, the flap of wings overhead, see the ever-changing colors of the Canadian sky. He experienced again the feeling of being part of a natural order, a 'child of the universe.' With his spirit revived, he printed out an attractive copy of the poem to have framed for Margie. He printed a simple copy to keep in his room. "This will help bolster me up when I'm feeling down."

His next stop was a frame shop where he found just the right one for Margie's copy, a stand-up frame, not too simple, not too ornate. He entered the house quietly, slipped into the parlor, and stood the framed poem on Margie's desk.

* * *

"Hey, Terry." Charlie peered around into the bay where Eric was replacing spark plugs in a 2009 Toyota Camry. "We're eating out for lunch. Wife's gone to check on her mother in an assisted living place in Fort Frances. Left early this morning, so no lunch bags today."

"Where are we going, Boss?"

"Just across the street, to the little KNK Brewery. Have you been there?"

"Once. Food's good."

They settled on stools at the bar. Charlie ordered cheeseburgers, fries, and two beers for them.

"Okay to have a beer while on the job?" Eric asked, surprised because of Charlie's experience with the last mechanic.

"I don't think I have anything to worry about. You're a pretty sober guy."

Eric watched the barman pour the frothy drafts and set them on the counter in front of them.

"You know, Charlie, I can't keep eating your wife's free lunches. I need to pay her."

"Not a problem. She enjoys making them. As a matter of fact, she keeps reminding me to invite you to dinner and I keep forgetting. Can you come over Friday night?"

Eric hesitated, again surprised. "I guess so. I'll have to let Margie know."

"Bring Margie with you. She has a car and knows where I live. That'll make it easy."

The burgers and fries arrived along with the bill which Eric grabbed before Charlie had a chance.

* * *

The dinner at Charlie Abbott's was hearty—braised beef, creamed potatoes, corn, green beans, dinner rolls and apple-raisin pie. Eric understood why Charlie's waist was enlarged, as was Mrs. Abbott's. He much preferred Margie's lighter, delicately seasoned meals. The conversation at table had centered around food, places to eat, and things to do in Kenora. At dessert Eric politely changed the subject."

"How is your mother, Mrs. Abbott?"

"About as well as can be expected. She has her aches and pains, but at least she's in a nice facility in Fort Frances and gets good care. I wish she were closer, though. Are your parents still with us, Mr. McElvin?"

"My father still lives in the Chicago area. My mother passed away a few years ago."

"You must regret being so far away from your family, especially if you have a wife and children. How long do you plan to stay in Kenora?"

Margie glanced at Eric then down at her pie plate.

"How about another piece of pie, Eric? Margie?" Charlie interrupted the inquisition.

"It's delicious but I can't eat another bite," Margie spoke up. "And I need to get back home to take some things out of the freezer for tomorrow. She pushed her chair back, Eric did likewise.

After all the "thank you's" and "good night's" were said Eric and Margie were grateful to be alone in the car.

"Charlie's wife has always been a little aggressive. Please don't let it bother you. You seem to be doing so well lately."

"I am. Thanks to you. And I enjoy being with Charlie."

"I'm glad. He's a good, strong man. He keeps *her* under control."

They both laughed.

Inside Margie's foyer, she turned the deadbolt then faced her companion.

"Terry, I have another place for you to visit this weekend, if you like old haunted houses."

"I've never encountered a haunted house I didn't like."

"There's a lovely Queen Anne Victorian mansion over in Keewatin that dates from the late eighteen hundreds, well maintained, and complete with period furniture. They say it's haunted. It's open to the public and they serve a wonderful tea on Sunday afternoon. Would you be interested?"

"Only if you accompany me."

"Well then, we have another date."

Eric stood at the bottom step and watched Margie walk down the hall to her bedroom leaving a trail of soft perfume which he inhaled before climbing the stairs.

* * *

"You've been in Kenora a month now, Terry. I hope it's beginning to feel like home."

Margie stirred a lump of sugar into her blueberry tea. She wore another of her well-chosen outfits: a light green silk blouse over tan loose-leg slacks fitted at the waist. "You are starting to seem like family. Even Josey said so the other day."

Eric didn't respond right away. He sat staring into the living room of the haunted mansion. He closed his eyes for a moment then turned toward Margie.

"Are there other guests for dinner tonight?"

"No, just the three of us. Why? Would you like to invite someone?"

Eric looked away then back again. "I would like to help clean up and talk with you afterwards, when Josey has gone back to her room or out with her friends."

"Of course. You seem so serious."

"I am. I want to tell you my story. Everything. Why I am here, why I am so secretive about my circumstances. It's getting harder and harder to repress the truth. And I believe I can trust you."

"You can, Terry, absolutely you can." She smiled without parting her lips, sincerity emanating from her eyes. By the way, you might like to know that Nancy Abbott called me yesterday, grilling me about you. I explained to her in no uncertain terms that it was my policy never to question my guests. I don't think she'll call back."

"Thank you, my fair lady."

They finished their tea and biscuits and completed the tour of the Mather-Walls house. On the way home Eric felt a weight gradually lifting from his heart as he pondered exactly how and what he would say to Margie after dinner.

That evening after the meal they sat in the parlor, Margie in an armchair, Eric on the sofa.

"Bear with me. It's a long story."

"I have all night."

He began by describing the state of his relationship with Sandy—how they had drifted so far apart, with Rebecca—how they had grown close despite his late hours, with his employees—how he enjoyed their company at work and at happy hour. He related in detail the night of the crime, explained how he became the prime suspect and summarized his brother's plan to buy him time. At that point he paused in the narrative.

"Could I have a glass of water, Margie?"

Without a word she went into the kitchen and came back with two glasses of an iced drink. She handed one to Eric.

"Water. With Crown Royal in it." Rather than settle back into the armchair, she sat perched on the edge of the seat, placed her drink on a side table.

"Please go on, Terry."

"Margie, my name is Eric. Eric Sanders, but continue to call me Terry." He took a sip of his drink before relating the details of his journey from Cinnamon Lake to Kenora: how he had to abandon his fishing partner who was being attacked by a bear, how the wilderness and its dwellers renewed his spirit in moments of fatigue and despair, how he used Darius' cabin and the UTV, and how he walked willingly into the unknown when he walked through her front door.

"If you want to alert the Mounties or whatever the police are called here, I understand. But I could not go on another day without telling you the truth."

Margie moved to the couch, took both of Eric's hands in hers.

"Terry—or Eric—you are truly an amazing man. You have endured the unbearable, you have lived through the impossible. I am so glad you are here and have shared all of this with me. I am your friend. I have become quite fond of you and you know that I will help you in any way I can."

Eric's throat tightened while a panoply of emotions flooded his soul. They sat in silence for a long time, Margie still holding Eric's hands. Droplets fell, making dark stains on the bodice of her light green blouse.

* * *

Eric awoke to the slapping of heavy rain on his windows. He did not relish walking the six blocks to work in this. But he had done it before and he would do it again. He pulled himself out of bed and went through the morning routine. He was downstairs early every day now. As usual Margie was there baking. Today she had donned a yellow ruffled apron so bright it seemed to smile and say 'Good Morning. It's a beautiful day!'

"Cinnamon rolls today, Terry."

"Well, good morning, Wonder Woman." Eric wanted the conversation at breakfast to be light and easy after the late-night confessional. She took the cue from him.

* * *

"Hey! You got a little wet, eh? You could have almost got here by boat!" Charlie's greeting to a soaked Eric. "Nancy sent you a thermos of hot chocolate to take the chill off."

"Bless Nancy!" Eric took the thermos and went into bay one. "Where'd the Ford Focus come from?"

"A guy brought it in early. I need you to check it out thoroughly."

"From headlights to tailpipe?"

"Exactly. Keys are in the ignition."

An hour later Eric returned to the office. "Charlie, I can't find anything that needs repairing on that little Focus. It's a nice car."

"That's good news for you, 'cause it's yours for as long as you need it."

"What are you saying?"

"I can't have my mechanic walking to work in bad weather. Besides, if you going to take Miss Margie around places, you'll need, as you said, a 'nice car.'"

"Whose car is it?"

"It's yours now."

"But I can't …"

"Yes, you can, and you will. I'm the boss here. Now there's work to be done in bay two."

The repair jobs were simple, at least for Eric. He finished around three and sauntered back into the office, waited until Charlie got off the phone.

"Now tell me about the Focus, seriously, Charlie. For all I know I could be driving a stolen car home today."

Charlie laughed. "It was a steal, actually. My wife's aunt died and the cousins were in a hurry to liquidate her property, so I offered three thousand for it. They took it. You saw the low mileage."

"Quite a deal. For a four-year-old car it looks brand new. Next you can tell me the true story on your '79 Ranchero."

"You saw the registration"

"I did."

"I just couldn't resist that beauty. Now get outta here! Go ride around town!"

* * *

Eric drove home in his newly-begotten Ford Focus. It felt good to sit behind the wheel again. He parked around back of the house but entered by the front door. In his room he opened the closet, retrieved his lock box, counted out the bills, and placed them in an envelope. On the front he wrote simply 'Margie. Terry's rent.' In her desk he found some cellophane tape and taped the envelope to the refrigerator door. Next he went to the phone in the parlor and called Eagle Rock Lodge to make dinner reservations for two Saturday evening.

The weather was too chilly for cocktails in the garden, but dinner in the restaurant was first class. Eric ordered steak, Margie went with scallops.

"This is my treat, Margie."

"Another thing to thank you for. The lovely framed Desiderata you placed on my desk, the envelope on the refrigerator, now this. Really, there was no rush to pay for next month."

"Don't want to lose my place at your table!"

During the meal several people stopped by their table to greet Margie. Each time she introduced them to her guest 'Terrence McElvin.'

They lingered over decaf coffee after dinner. During the drive home a light snow was falling. Eric left the Focus parked in front of the house, put his jacket around her shoulders and escorted Margie to the door. Once inside the foyer, she slipped his jacket on the coat rack. They said the usual thank you's and goodnight's at the bottom of the stairs. Eric put one hand on Margie's waist and drew her to him. The kiss was long and deep— an expression of passion that grew out of trust, gratitude and just plain need for someone. They both pulled away.

"We can't, Terry... Eric."

"I know. It's too soon since ... But I'm not sorry."

"Neither am I."

Chapter Fourteen
Chicago

"Where's the other half of my money? You know what we agreed—half up front and half after the job. I'm sick of waiting. It's been over a month now. That's laying low long enough."

"Right. Half *after* the hit. When are you going to get off your rear end and do it?"

"It's done already. I guarantee you. She's real dead."

"What are you trying to pull? She's very much alive. I saw her this morning—with the boyfriend."

"No way. I went into that house and offed her. By the way, you didn't tell me about the kid."

"What kid? There is no kid."

"And the back door opens into a laundry room, not the kitchen."

"Wai … ait a minute. Which house did you go in?"

"What do you mean which house? The one at the address you gave me. 431 Oak Park Drive."

"Oak *Park?* God, you moron! It's Oak *Bark*! Oak Park isn't anywhere near where she lives! It's 431 Oak Bark Drive. Look at the slip of paper I gave you!"

"Can't. I memorized the address and destroyed the paper."

"So you went into the wrong house and you shot the wrong woman!"

"I didn't shoot her. I used a knife."

"What the …! This is getting unbelievable. Of all people, I would pick an idiot for this.

So, are you going to do the job? If not I want my ten thousand back."

"You're just claiming this to weasel out of paying me the rest. I want my other ten grand, now!"

"Then you have forty-eight hours or I'll hire somebody with a brain to take *you and her* out!"

Click

Sam stood with the cell phone still to his ear. His mind was turning somersaults. '*You went into the wrong house and shot the wrong woman.*' He pictured the woman standing at the door with her child. He could hear her in the kitchen saying "Eric, is that you?" He thought about that. The husband hired him and his name is not Eric. The woman probably wouldn't say her lover's name since it might be her husband coming in for something.

"Geez. Maybe I did kill the wrong woman. No, the guy's lying. Never heard of Oak Bark Drive."

He opened a drawer in the kitchenette and consulted his map *Chicago and the Suburbs*. Listed in the street guide he found *Oak Avenue, Oak Lane, Oak Street, Oak Bark Drive, Oak Branch Circle, ... Oak Park Drive*. He checked the coordinates for Oak Bark. Way to the south of Oak Park. As the truth began to dawn on him, fear like a black widow spider crawled from his brain, down his spine, and spun her web inside him.

He opened a drawer in the kitchenette and consulted his map *Chicago and the Suburbs*. Listed in the street guide he found *Oak Avenue, Oak Lane, Oak Street, Oak Bark Drive, Oak Branch Circle, . . . Oak Park Drive*. He checked the coordinates for Oak Bark. Way to the south of Oak Park. As the truth began to dawn on him, fear like a black widow spider crawled from his brain, down his spine, and spun her web inside him.

"He can't be right. I can't believe I killed the wrong woman. A wife. A mother. I shoudda kept that paper with the address. All because I was trying to be so careful. Leave no trace. I'm a professional. I have to be careful."

All he wanted right now was bourbon, more than one belt of it.

* * *

"Well, well! As I live and breathe. The Sherlock Holmes of Chi-town. Are you still sleuthing around?"

"Ever since I retired from the force."

"What brings you back to these hallowed halls?"

"I come bearing gifts." He tossed two plastic evidence bags on Trexler's desk. "For the Sanders case. I think I've found your perp."

"You mean Eric Sanders?"

"Wrong. His name is Samuel Clark. He lives in a seedy apartment building on Billows Avenue where a dumpster diver found the bloody gloves and cloth." He pointed to the plastic bags on Trexler's desk. I had an old friend in the department—who shall remain nameless—run tests and found the blood matches Sandra Sanders. The teenage boy, who lives next door to the Sanders, and who is really into cars, saw a black late-model Toyota Altima parked in front of their house the night of the murder. It was gone the next morning."

"Whoa, slow down a minute. Is all this documented?"

"It is. What's more, a car matching that description is sitting, as we speak, in the parking lot on Billows Avenue. Registered to a Samuel A. Clark, who also lives in the building, an old hotel converted into tiny apartments. Residents are mostly transients. Stay for a month or two. Management doesn't do background checks. I suggest you get a search warrant for both the apartment and the car—check it with luminol. And you'll need one for sleazy Sam's arrest."

"How did you come by this dumpster evidence?" Trexler's brow furrowed up like a Sharpei dog's face as he picked up one of the bags.

"I still have friends in low places."

"And high places. I take it you're working for Alan Sanders."

"He pays well. Oh, almost forgot. The lock on the back door of the Sanders home was picked. I think your guys missed that. Plus there were footprints outside in the freshly-cut grass by the bushes that were nowhere near the size that Eric wears. I guess they missed that, too. So I'd say Eric Sanders did not kill his wife."

"And all this is documented?"

The investigator handed Trexler a thick file folder. "See for yourself." He stood and turned to go.

"You can thank me later."

Once the investigator left, Trexler leafed through the file then sat and read it thoroughly. It was all there, documented.

"Damn, he's good. And I look like a fool." He picked up the phone. "This is Trexler. Get me Judge Schuler. I need a couple of warrants."

* * *

His head throbbed like it had been between cymbals during a Souza march. His throat and mouth would make the Gobi Desert seem like a tropical paradise. Sam was out of whiskey, out of food, and most importantly, out of money. He had used the income from his first hit plus the advance on this one to pay cash for the Nissan. There was little or nothing left. He had enjoyed a three-day bender to celebrate his stabbing of *the wrong woman. Wrong house, wrong woman.* The alcohol helped temporarily get the images out of his mind: The dim figures of a mother and child standing in the front door. The knife in her hand. The Eiffel Tower apron. Her voice. The kid's voice.

It took Sam a minute to realize that someone was knocking at the door.

"Mr. Clark, it's the manager. I need to speak to you."

Sam glanced around for his gun. Couldn't remember what he did with it.

"Yeah? What do you want?"

"You're a week late on the rent. You have to pay on time or you're out. That's the rule. I've got prospective tenants waiting."

"I'm sick in bed right now. I'll bring it to the office tomorrow."

"Tomorrow by noon or you're on the street."

"Okay, okay. I hear you." Sam sat on the couch, head hanging. "Two deadlines. Noon tomorrow or I'm back on the streets. Forty-eight hours or I'm dead. Have to find 431 Oak *Bark* and do the job. Again." Sam pulled himself up, found the Chicago map, located Oak Bark Drive and circled it. Another knock at the door.

"I said okay! I'll pay tomorrow! By noon!"

"Samuel Clark, Chicago Police. We have a search warrant. Open the door or we're coming in."

* * *

Trexler sat on a rolling desk chair facing a twitchy Sam Clark in a straight-backed wooden one. A sharp-faced policewoman who had the demeanor of a robocop sat at a small table with recording equipment. The sparse furnishings of the interview room were a necessary precaution against any attempt at violence. Besides, the lieutenant liked it that way. He felt more in command. Trexler glanced at robocop and she switched on the recorder.

"State your full name."

"Samuel Austin Clark"

"Do you know why you're here?"

"I have no idea."

"Do you know a Sandra or Eric Sanders?"

"Never heard of them."

"How about the address 431 Oak Park Drive?"

The spider tightened her web of fear. *God, how could they know?*

"Denial will do you no good, Clark. We found the gloves and cloth you disposed of in the dumpster. The blood on them is Sandra Sanders,' as are the blood traces we found in your Altima. We have two witnesses who can put you at the scene of the crime—a teenage boy who lives next door and the Sanders' daughter." Trexler threw that little exaggeration in for good measure.

Sam did not respond right away. He sat perspiring.

"You might as well confess to the murder and life will be much easier for you. The judge will be more lenient. Why did you kill her?" Trexler rolled his chair closer. "She was an attractive woman. Had you been lusting after her and she rejected your advances? Or was this a random thrill kill. You saw her and thought you could get off on stabbing her multiple times."

Sam fidgeted in his seat. A river of sweat ran from each temple.

"I told you I don't know her! I never saw her before!" He was panicking. "I was hired to do it!"

Trexler rolled back. "And who hired you? Was it Eric Sanders? Was it? I'll ask you again. Was it Eric Sanders? Tell us and we can offer you a deal."

"I need a lawyer."

"We'll be glad to provide you with one, but I'll tell you this: he will advise you to take the plea bargain: a reduced sentence with eventual eligibility for parole or else life in prison without the possibility of parole. You have to decide. If you go to trial, the DA will dig up everything in your past and use it against you." Trexler stood. "Sergeant," he called to the officer outside the door. "Take him to a cell. We going to hold him for further questioning."

"No, wait. I'll tell you, I'll tell you it was all a big mistake, *my* mistake. I just made a mistake. A simple little mistake, that's all," Sam sobbed.

Trexler listened to Sam's confession, all the details. He was surprised how easily the man broke. Now he had two suspects: Sam Clark and the person who hired him. Eric Sanders was completely innocent of murdering his wife.

After the session with Sam, Trexler sat at his desk shaking his head." Oak Park, Oak Bark. Such a small thing to make a huge difference in so many lives.

Trexler didn't sleep well that night. The case was full of details that had to be taken care of before it could be presented to the District Attorney. They had to be precise and accurate. He worried about using the teenage boy and the Sanders' daughter to coerce a confession. The next morning he was at his desk in the precinct earlier than usual. Robocop had already placed a copy of the interview on his desk. He wondered how he could cut out the part about the boy and girl. The morning was spent scrutinizing everything to do with the case.

He was about to break for lunch when his phone rang.

"Lieutenant Trexler, this is Meredith Marsten at Baldwin Lake Lodge in Canada. I have located Eric Sanders."

"I'm listening."

"In your phone call you mentioned a satellite map that showed a clearing near Wheeler Lake and thought Eric could have been picked up by helicopter there and flown to Winnipeg."

"That's correct. I alerted the Manitoba Mounties and they are seeking his whereabouts in the city and surrounding area."

"Well, he's not in Winnipeg. He's in Kenora, Ontario."

"What makes you say that?"

"I remembered a few years ago a company in Ontario set up a logging camp there and felled trees for a couple of years until the Manitoba government put a stop to it. They must have cut a logging road connecting the camp to somewhere in Ontario. I checked with the company and, sure enough, there is a logging road that runs past Wheeler Lake and finally reaches an unmarked dirt road which becomes a two-lane black top that passes through an aboriginal settlement and eventually connects to highway 17 and Kenora. I called my colleague Kevin Walsten—he's an outfitter who flies out of Kenora. He told me he had met a Terrence McElvin. He then asked around and found that McElvin was staying at a Margaret Taylor's rooming house. I have that number for you. I didn't consider it my place to go any further."

This was another bolt out of the blue for Trexler. Yesterday the evidence bags from a private investigator, today Sanders located by a young lady operating a Canadian fishing and hunting lodge. He cleared his throat. "Thank you for that consideration. And the number?" Trexler grabbed a pen, scribbled down the number, and thanked Meredith for her detective work and the call before hanging up.

"It seems that other people are doing my job for me. Maybe I should retire and start fishing in Canada." He sat trying to decide what his next step should be. He perused the Sanders case file which still lay open on his desk and found what he wanted. He picked up the phone and punched in the office number of a wealthy business CEO. As he expected, a recorded message answered. "You've reached the executive offices of Fidelity Investments. Please leave your name, number, and a brief message and your call will be returned within one business day." "This is Lieutenant Trexler of the Chicago Police Department. I need to speak with Alan Sanders as soon as possible. He has my card and number."

* * *

Kathy was doing her best to reassure Rebecca. At first, taking her to a movie, the zoo, a shopping mall, an ice cream parlor, a skating rink, or anywhere she could think of, kept her happy and kept the questions about Mom and Dad to a minimum. But after a month, new places, new clothes, and new experiences could not fill the void. Rebecca wanted to know where they were, why they went, when they were coming back. Kathy had mastered giving vague answers to these questions, but it was difficult to formulate a convincing answer to Why haven't they called me? Why haven't they texted me? Or, why can't they do Skype or Zoom?

"Your daddy is on a secret mission for the government in a foreign country and can't reveal where he is to anyone."

"Your Mommy is so busy taking care of her sick cousin who lives in a rural area with no internet, no phone lines or cell phone towers."

The answers temporarily relieved the questioning but added to the child's growing unhappiness and withdrawal. She now spent almost all her time in her room—a guest bedroom converted into a child's dream room with a princess canopy bed and dresser, a pile of stuffed animals, laptop computer, TV with DVD's appropriate for a ten-year-old. Her appetite, hearty at the beginning, had waned. She asked to be excused from the table, most of her food still on the plate.

The *coup de grace* came one night when Kathy found her crying with heaves and sobs the way one cries when grieving. "What is it, Sweetie? Why are you so sad?"

"My Mom and Dad are gone forever! I'll never see either of them again! I'm an orphan now!"

"No, Becca, no. That's not true! You have parents and relatives who love you very much! We're going to celebrate your birthday soon and invite your friends for a party."

"I don't have any friends here! They're all over in Oak Park! I'll never see them again either!"

Kathy realized the inadequacy of any words she might say. The child was inconsolable. The long separation had worn her patience too thin. She put her arms around the girl and held her close until despair had abated and tears ceased for now.

* * *

"Lieutenant Trexler, Alan Sanders here returning your call. Let me save you the time and trouble: No, I have not heard from nor seen Eric and no, I do not know where he is."

"Actually, Mr. Sanders, I *do* know where he is. I'm calling to tell you that he can come home now without fear of incarceration. He will not be indicted for the murder of his wife. We have arrested and charged the perpetrator. He has confessed to the crime, so there will not even be a trial."

"Are you telling me that Eric is a free man now?"

"That is exactly what I'm telling you. I have the phone number of the rooming house where he is staying in Kenora, Ontario. I thought you might prefer to be the one to give him the news rather than the police."

"Please tell me who murdered Sandra."

"A hired killer who entered the Sanders home by mistake. I'll fill you in on the details later. Right now call Eric and get him home."

"This is so unbelievable and . . . so unexpected. Thank you, Lieutenant for your work in solving this."

"I can't take the credit. Thank your PI and Meredith Marsten at Baldwin Lake Lodge. They did the sleuth work."

"Well then, thank you for allowing me to be the one to tell Eric."

"When he gets back, we will need to see him at the station. Formalities, you understand."

"I understand." He hung up. *It's over. This nightmare is over.*

Alan removed a drawer from his desk, found a piece of paper with a number on it taped to the underside. He called. A woman's voice answered.

"Margaret Taylor's Rooms and Meals. This is Margie."

"I need to speak to Terrence McElvin, please."

"He's at work now. May I take a message?"

"Tell him it's Alan, his brother. And tell him he's free to come home now."

Chapter Fifteen
Cinnamon Lake

Six weeks after the bear attack

"Okay, guys. Get on board for your flight over to Cinnamon Lake. Bows in the back, butts on the back seats. I'm riding shotgun." The two hunters followed instructions, climbed into the Cessna seaplane, took their seats, and fastened safety belts. "My name is Wayne Coburn, certified bear hunting guide in Ontario and Manitoba. Mark Redcloud hired me to be your guide for this week's hunt. Your pilot will be the lovely Meredith Marsten, co-owner and manager of Baldwin Lake Lodge. Now don't get any ideas. She's Mark's wife." The guide continued to give orders and information while Meredith made sure the door was shut tight before putting on headphones and preparing for take-off. The noise of the four-seater seaplane's engine made further conversation impossible.

Gaining speed on the surface of Baldwin Lake caused the floats to push up a wall of spray that formed a curtain on each side of the plane. Once airborne the curtain disappeared and the irregular shapes created by the whims of Nature stretched out in all directions. Left undisturbed, the lower taiga forest seen from the air became a spectacle of jigsaw-puzzle-shaped lakes with rivers and streams drawn in fanciful curves and angles. The hunters and even the guide seemed fascinated by the view from on high. Meredith, who had always flown by visual rules, knew the landscape by heart and used it the way drivers use highway signs.

After a smooth landing on Cinnamon Lake, the pilot performed her one-man docking routine and helped the three passengers climb down out of the plane. The men unloaded their luggage onto the dock—duffles, sleeping bags, groceries, and weapons. Last but not least, the cartons of Labatt's Blue beer.

"Good luck, guys. Be extremely careful. Bear hunting is a bit more dangerous than deer hunting! I'll be back in a couple of days to check on you. There is a satellite phone with instructions in the cabin. Don't hesitate to use it if any problem should arise." With that reassurance Meredith and the seaplane taxied out, gained momentum and lifted off, leaving the hunters and guide to their week in the wilderness.

"First things first. Let's get this beer in the fridge." Wayne hoisted a case of twenty-four beers and headed to the cabin. The two hunters followed suit. Once the beers were safely stashed and chilling, each man brought his gear in.

"I've picked my bunk. The others are up for grabs." Wayne popped the tab on a beer.

"Today we'll just settle in, get to know each other, and plan out our week. On the central table he spread out a map of the Cinnamon Lake area which Meredith had provided. The others joined him, beer in hand.

"I thought we'd set our bait station here." He pointed to an "X" mark just off the path to Wheeler Lake. "I understand there's been some bear activity in this spot. Now let's sit down and I want you guys to tell me your names. I have them written in my notes, but I'd like to hear from both of you about where you live, your family, your jobs. We're going to be depending on each other for safety here, so I think we need to get pretty well acquainted."

"I'm Rick Morrison and this is my friend Jim Holbrooke. We're both from Saint Paul, Minnesota and work together in the offices of Prudential Insurance." Each hunter shook hands with the guide.

"Any kids?"

"I have a boy twelve years old who already loves to fish and hunt," Jim spoke up.

"And I have twin girls eight years old, blond and beautiful," Rick added. "What about you?"

"Two grown sons and an ex-wife." Wayne took off his camo cap, ran a hand over his army-style graying buzz cut, and replaced the cap. "Like I said in the plane, I'm Wayne Coburn. Now that we know who we all are, let's do some planning and maybe a little target practice to get things going. First, I want to teach you the three A's of bear hunting: be *alert* at all times, be *accurate* when you shoot, and be *aware* of your teammates. And here's the reason we need to know each other: Bear hunting is an exciting but dangerous sport. You need to be convinced that no matter what happens you can trust and depend on your teammates."

So the men spent the day showing off their new compound bows, talking about techniques for the best shots, and shooting at trees, little knowing they were being closely observed by a large, black forest-dweller.

* * *

Kuru had taken a long and lazy morning stroll along his favorite lakeshore. He enjoyed some water plants that had washed up on the beach and even found a dead walleye which he devoured. He paused several times during his walk to sniff the air for telltale aromas. Nothing that aroused his instinct to hunt. Later today he perhaps would look for a ground runner or a longear, but right now he was content being by the water with the bright skylight warming his fur.

Then he heard something that made him prick up his ears. The roaring bird. He knew it would fly to the uprights' nest where it would sit on the surface of the water and let a few uprights out. He had to see if they were bringing firesticks, the one thing Kuru feared. He waited and listened to be sure of what he heard then turned and went back to his lake access path. A short distance from the shore it connected with the path that led to the uprights' nest. He headed in that direction, driven by curiosity. His stride was shorter, his gait brisker.

He used a familiar spot behind a group of young poplars and tall bramble bushes where he could watch the uprights without being seen. They were carrying bundles into the nest when he arrived and the roaring bird's nose was turning and whirring, which Kuru knew meant it was about to rise toward the sky. Once all the bundles and things were inside and the bird had disappeared into the clouds, there was only silence. Kuru waited. He smelled some late blackberries still growing on the bush he had his nose in, so he ate them.

After a long wait Kuru, despite his urgent curiosity, felt sleepy. Just as he was about to nod off, the uprights came out holding strange-looking objects that resembled small, twisted branches. They put sticks in them and the sticks would fly out and lodge in tree trunks or the ground. He had seen many uprights with long poles and strings go out in water skimmers and catch swimmers, but this was new for Kuru. He watched for quite a while but could not understand what they were doing or why. "The uprights are certainly strange creatures. I need to stay nearby to see what they will do with the stick-throwers."

He backed out of his hiding place. Circling around to the other side of the big nest, he ran across a ground runner and played chase for a while until he grew tired of the game, pierced its neck with his claws and ate it. But all the while his mind was mainly on the uprights. He didn't trust them, he didn't want to engage with them, in fact, he preferred to stay clear of them. Still, he studied them. He understood everything that happened in this his forestial territory. He knew the habits of all its creatures, those of the land and those of the sky. He knew the growing things of the earth; he knew the seasons and the signs of change. Everything was regular and ordered. In his world he could survive and be content. He could live without fear. Nothing could harm him … except the firesticks. The uprights' firesticks. That is why he had to watch them and try to figure things out.

He found a comfortable place for a nap and settled down, but a crow kept screaming at him. That annoyed him, so he moved away and found another place. Skywater began to fall on him. It was cold but not white. He closed his eyes. He could still hear any sounds coming from the nest, so this was a good place to sleep until fading light time.

* * *

Rick felt surprisingly good about his practice shoot yesterday. He had not been hunting in a few weeks. He had fared well in last year's deer season and the freezer was full of venison. Likewise for Jim. At lunch break one day the idea of a bear hunt this fall came up.

"It would be a once-in-a-lifetime thrill, for sure," Jim said. "Are you game? No pun intended."

"Let's give it a shot, no pun intended here either!"

Rick valued his light-hearted camaraderie with Jim, but he knew a bear hunt would test the extent of their friendship. He had read several books about bears and spent hours online researching information and advice on successful bear hunting. The two frequently went target practicing together. He hoped he was ready. And here they were in the middle of the Canadian wilderness with a pushy guide, lots of beer, and their lives possibly depending on each one's skill with bow and arrow.

"No rush this morning, gentlemen." Wayne helped himself to two packets of instant oatmeal, emptied them into a bowl, poured hot water over the contents, and sat down with the hunters for their allotted breakfast. "Today we build our blinds around noon. We're using natural resources to make them ground-level."

"Not tree blinds?" Jim asked.

"Nope. The angle for a death shot from a tree requires much more skill and accuracy. This is your first bear hunt, so you need to be closer and level with the animal's heart and lungs. You definitely don't want to wound a black bear and make him angry. They are great climbers, so a tree wouldn't protect you."

Rick and Jim exchanged glances.

"Even though you'll be under cover, the bear will smell you and hear the slightest movement. So he will know you're there, but probably not consider you a threat. Unlike the spoiled bears of the national parks in the States, here in the taiga forest black bears prefer to stay away from humans. So bank on that. Now here are some sketches of natural blinds." Wayne took a piece of paper from an inside pocket of his camo jacket and laid it before the men. "You see the logs set up teepee style against a tree with foliage in between. So around noon we'll go out, gather our materials, and get set up. Bears are most active at dawn and dusk. No need to be jittery. I'll be there with my rifle. Okay, one other thing. When we go out this afternoon, don't bring any food or snacks, but do bring a closed container for your urine. Any questions?"

"What do we use for bait?" Rick asked.

"The lodge has supplied us with several bricks of bacon lard, which bears love. I'll take care of putting it out and set up a nice dinner table for ole' Bruno!"

The men spent three hours setting up their bait site with blinds. First they portaged supplies from the cabin to the spot Wayne had chosen. It was not a clearing but the trees and shrubs were sparse enough. Then they searched out five- or six-foot logs and leafy branches to construct the blinds. The guide provided each hunter with a small camp stool, the last item to add.

"You will be sitting where you have full view of the bait and of each other. If the bear approaches the bait or your partner's blind, you will have a perfect shot. Remember to aim behind the shoulders midbody. The arrow should go in, pierce the heart and lungs, and come out the other side. If you mess up your shot and anger the bear, he may come at you. But I will position myself to have a clear shot. You have a partner with a bow and me with a rifle, so don't panic. In all case scenarios I've got your back."

The men ate a couple of energy bars then positioned themselves, each in his blind. Wayne set out the bait then lay prone a little farther back behind a hillock. He began blowing a dying rabbit bear call.

They waited, listening to every tiny sound in the forest. A raccoon arrived and inspected the bait. The wind picked up. Rick couldn't decide whether he was upwind or downwind of the bait and any bear eating at it.

"One of us is going to get that bear . . . and I hope it doesn't have to be Wayne with the rifle." Rick's attention went to his Garmin LED site attached to his bow. As he checked it out he felt a rush of adrenaline when his mind pictured a bear through his site. "When he comes, I will not be afraid. I will shoot with deadly accuracy."

At first the time went quickly. As the light began to dim, Rick's stomach told him it was suppertime. The minutes dragged by until Rick heard Wayne call out. Okay, men, enough for today. Push a log down and get out. Take your stool with you then put the log back up."

Wayne was not a gourmet chef. Scrambled eggs and instant grits tasted good, but the beer tasted a lot better. Rick's sleep was filled with visions of bears, one behind a tree, then one at the bait, another peering in between the logs and branches) that camouflaged him. He woke up sweating. Lying in his bunk he dealt with and defeated his fear, replacing it with a stiff determination. "I am going to kill that bear!"

The next day he spotted a bear through the distant trees but it did not come near the bait. "Three days and no luck." Still Rick was determined and convinced he would bag a bear. On the fourth day a sow with a cub wandered in, ate for a while at the bait. Not a shot was taken. The morning of the fifth day Rick had an uncanny feeling. "Today is the day! I will get him at dusk today!" So he spent a patient morning in the blind, knowing his time would come later.

* * *

Jim's patience was wearing thin. Fifth day and no bear—or rather not one they could take out. Not a female with cub. But it was exciting to be so close to them. He really, really wanted to show his son a picture of his dad with a bear he bagged, maybe even bring home the head and hide. He and Rick had mutually decided no trophy from the hunt if they were successful. But still …being up close and personal with a mama and her baby made Jim wish he could share the experience with his son. He looked at his watch. Another hour before Wayne okayed lunch: two energy bars consumed in the blind.

It had rained intermittently days two, three, and four. The forest was so quiet you could hear rainwater dripping from the tall white pines and poplars. The distant bellow of a bull moose gave Jim perspective on his situation: except for his bow and arrows, he was a weak, defenseless creature in the face of those much better provided for by Mother Nature, those much better adapted to the harsh environment of the wilderness. They possessed keen senses and instincts that served them well. Jim was overwhelmed by the immensity and complexity of pristine nature, yet amazed by the beauty of it, the infinite variety of its flora and fauna, each with its own distinctive characteristics.

"I must bring my son here so that he can experience for himself the awe of nature and the excitement of the hunt. A photo of me and a dead bear is not terribly inspiring."

Jim's meditation was interrupted by Wayne's lost cub bear call.

"That may bring Mama Bear back. Maybe Papa Bear will join her." He wondered if the afternoon would be as long and fruitless as the morning. Something told him it wouldn't be. He sat up straight and checked his sight at the sound of something big and heavy moving through the woods, coming toward the bait. His throat tightened and nerve endings in his hands and arms began to burn. He had to keep telling himself to breathe normally and maintain control. He nocked an arrow and readied his fingers for the draw.

* * *

Rick heard the movement in the brush and for a second glimpsed a large black figure between the trees. "It's him!" His system went into high speed. Rapid breathing, pulse racing. The bear came into full view as it approached the bait. Through the site Rick had a clear shot behind the shoulders. Arrow ready, he pulled and released.

When the arrow struck, the bear instantly leaped up, all fours in the air like he was jumping over a hurdle. Instead of running back the way he came, he loped toward Rick's blind. Jim knew his partner was in danger but didn't have time to think. He aimed and took his shot. The bear again leaped into the air, then started running fast toward dense cover.

Rick's heart pounded. "Thank God Jim was alert."

"Go after him! Stay on his trail. Find the blood trail!" Wayne was standing with rifle aimed. Rick and Jim pushed out of the blinds and took the direction of the wounded bear, following the broken bushes and crushed foliage. Moving through the dense forest wasn't easy going. They lost sight and sound of him for a while.

"Blood here!" Rick yelled. They were on his trail again. As the blood drops became more profuse the men slowed their pace.

"He's not far now," Wayne had taken the lead.

There was a noise, a cry, a long, loud wailing that rose and fell in pitch. The men stopped to listen.

"The death moan," Wayne told his archers. "You got him."

They found the body fallen at the base of a tree with deep scratch marks on the trunk. From what he had read in preparation for the hunt Rick knew the grooves served two purposes: to sharpen claws and to mark territory. He felt a pang of guilt. "We invaded his territory and killed him. He never did any harm."

"Not true," Wayne said. "I think this is the bear that mauled a fisherman a few weeks ago. See this bad scar?" Wayne turned the head to one side with his foot. "You guys did a good thing taking him down. Now let's get some pictures to bring home."

* * *

The uprights left the nest early. Kuru had already taken his stroll along the shore before first light and eaten his fill of plants and insects. Then he heard them moving down the path that goes to the little lake, making no attempt to be undetected. He followed at a distance. He saw them pulling fallen logs up and placing them against a tree. This bothered him. "They are disturbing my food! The bugs will bury themselves deeper. Impossible for me to pull in with my tongue." They tore branches off bushes and put them with the logs. "What are they doing? Building another nest? Two more little nests?" Again Kuru felt frustrated not understanding the uprights. He had grown accustomed to the ones with poles and long strings that went in water skimmers to pull swimmers from the lake. He realized they wanted them for food, although they put most of them back into the water. But these doings with the logs and branches made no sense to Kuru.

For several light cycles they would come out of the big nest and go into the little ones, carrying the twisted sticks with them. They seem to be guarding a container of something to eat. Kuru could smell it and wanted it, but he followed his instincts and stayed away. When he saw the female bear that shared his territory go to the food with her cub and eat some, he couldn't help himself. He had to get some, too. The white season was close, so he needed to eat all he possibly could.

The next light cycle, well before last light, Kuru carefully approached the area of little nests and the food container. The aroma of the food was irresistible. It reeked of fatty meat, just what he craved. He reached the container and began to lick the chunk of food. He heard a whirr and something hit his side, hard. His body leaped into the air, all fours off the ground but he quickly regained control. He knew the blow came from one of the little nests and he started toward it. Another whirr, another hard hit, another leap into the air.

"Something is wrong! I have to get away from the stick-throwers!" Kuru ran into the shelter of the bushes and thickness of his forest. "The uprights are coming after me!" For the first time he felt danger, he felt what it was like to be the prey. Instinctively he headed for his sleeping place where he was sure he would be alright. He tried to run faster but strength was failing him. He had trouble taking in air. Despite his efforts, he was slowing down. By the time he reached the sleeping place, the forest was spinning around. He fell beside his special tree. The woods grew dim. He realized the life force was slipping away from him. He let out a long cry of desperation. Then there was darkness, complete darkness. Then there was nothingness, complete nothingness.

Chapter Sixteen
Emails

Rick to Meredith

Hello Ms. Marsten,

Just got home from the bear hunt at Cinnamon Lake. Jim and I appreciate you flying us in and out. You are a great pilot—and a pretty one, too! You asked us to send photos if the hunt was successful. Well it certainly was! We didn't need but two arrows and both were perfectly placed so the bear didn't stand a chance.

You found an excellent guide for us. Wayne was attentive to every detail to make sure we were all safe. He was demanding and his method was not always conventional but it worked. He gave us tips that made the difference and really paid off.

We thought about bringing the hide and head back home with us for a bearskin rug, but the brute (and he was enormous—probably 500 lbs.) had a real bad scar on the left side of his face just under the eye, so we left him to Mother Nature. I hope that's okay.

I have attached some pics for you. Sorry we didn't bag a more photogenic bruin for your use in a future publicity brochure.

It was the thrill of a lifetime. But I hope I'm never that scared again! Thanks again for providing us with this unforgettable opportunity.

Rick Morrison

* * *

Meredith to Rick

Hi Rick,

Congratulations on your successful bear hunt! And thanks for the photos. You did get a large *ursus americanus*. In fact you brought down a bear that professional hunters had failed to trap or kill. He had attacked one of the fishermen staying at Cinnamon Lake a few weeks ago. So, many thanks for that.

We are here if you ever decide to go bear hunting again—or moose hunting—or trophy walleye, pike, and lake trout fishing. I'm sending you a link in case you would like to download our newest brochure. No bear picture, but a nice bull moose and a lot of trophy fish shots.

Until next time?

Meredith Marsten

* * *

Jake to Billy

Hey Billy,

Hope you are 100% recovered from surgery and find yourself in pre-bear condition, except maybe for a few scars. I know we are planning to go fishing again at Cinnamon Lake next year, but let me propose something to you. How about deep-sea fishing out of Key West, Fla? At a friend's house recently I met a guy who just got back and he said it was phenomenal. Caught a 250-lb Blue Marlin! He gave me the name and number of a charter boat captain who will cut us a real deal. There's a non-stop flight to Miami. We rent a car at the airport and drive down the keys. Wonderful weather, fresh air, fresh orange juice, sea breezes, huge fish, and no bears. What say you? I've never tried salt-water fishing, but the guy highly recommended it. Think it over and get back to me when you have a chance. Canada or Florida? Whichever you decide will be fine with me. Just want to get something big on the end of my line!

Your friend and fishing buddy,

Jake

P.S. Before you make a decision, you should read Hemmingway's *Old Man and the Sea.*

* * *

Billy to Jake

Hey Jake,

I'm doing okay. Most of the scars are hidden under my clothes, so I look like nothing ever happened. But I don't feel that way! The trip to Florida and fishing in Key West sounds great and I'd like to do that maybe next year. But this year I need to go back to where it happened. It's the only way I know to get rid of the fear that haunts me. I have always loved the outdoors, especially the wilderness, and most especially the Canadian boreal forest. I don't want the bear to take that away from me. So I must face it, the sooner the better. I hope you understand and will go along with me. I promise our next adventure will be way down in the Florida Keys catching marlins, sharks, barracudas, and who knows what!
Your good buddy,

Billy

Eric to Baldwin Lake Lodge

To the lodge managers/ owners,

In all humility I ask your forgiveness for the worry and expense I brought upon you by disappearing from your outpost at Cinnamon Lake without explanation. I thought I was fleeing for my life. As you know by now, that was not the case. There is no way I can make up for the hours and manpower that was spent trying to find me. To make matters worse, I fled leaving a colleague being mauled by a bear. I will forever feel remorse for that. I hope you can find it in your hearts to pardon my careless desperation. I have heard that the attacking bear has been put down. I know you are relieved about that.

Getting on with my life, I would very much like to bring my daughter, who just turned 11, to one of your outposts (preferably not Cinnamon Lake!). She is eager to learn the art of fishing and I want her to experience the wonders of the Canadian boreal forest. Could you find a place for us next summer? I promise neither of us will disappear! I await your kind reply.

Eric Sanders ("Terrence McElvin")

P.S. A lady friend from Kenora, Ontario, may be joining us.

* * *

Baldwin Lake Lodge to Eric

Dear Eric,

We are certainly relieved not only that the dangerous bear has been put down but also that you were located safe and sound and are now reunited with your family.

Of course we will have a spot for you and your daughter next summer. I have you down tentatively for June 15 – 22. That is prime fishing time, so both of you should catch an abundance of fish—big ones! Let me know if those dates work for you. I am putting you in Poplar River outpost. It is a very special place that has a lot of history. Many people who have stayed there say it is enchanting and return year after year. Others say it is romantic. My mother and father spent their honeymoon there, and I am the result!

Meredith Marsten

Co-owner/co-manager

Baldwin Lake Lodge

* * *

Eric to Margie

Dear Margie,

It is an incredible joy to be with my daughter again. The reunion was quite emotional for both of us. I had to explain her mother's death. She is dealing with it, but it's tough. I have been telling her about my experiences in Canada. She loves the stories about my wild animal encounters and she wants to visit Kenora and meet "Miss Margie," as she calls you.

Words are not adequate to express the gratitude I owe you. You are an amazing and beautiful woman. You made my grief and isolation bearable. The times we spent together were happy ones. I think we have a very special relationship that I hope will continue.

I would love for you to get to know Rebecca and my brother Alan and his wife Kathy. It's an easy flight from Winnipeg to Chicago. Do consider a visit soon!

I send greetings to Josey. Tell her I wish her well as she begins her college years. Aren't we lucky to have such great daughters? I have attached a recent photo of Becca. Could you send one of Josey?

So many things I miss. I miss Kenora, my room and your delicious meals. I miss working with Charlie and I miss Nancy's lunches. Most of all I miss the lovely proprietress of *Margie's Rooms and Meals.*

With warm affection,

Eric aka Terry

Margie to Eric

Dear Eric aka Terry,

So glad you are with your sweet Rebecca again. With her mother gone in such a tragic way, she needs you to be both parents now. Thank you so much for sending along a photo of her. She is absolutely beautiful!

I hope everything is okay at your auto shop and that your replacement handled the business well for you. Charlie is still looking for a good mechanic. He says he will never be able to replace you, but he's getting by.

A visit to Chicago is enticing. To have an occasion to meet your family would be a pleasure. As you can imagine, it would be difficult for me to leave the responsibility of the house and guests to someone else. I will try to work something out. For my part, I would like to invite you and Rebecca to visit Kenora during winter holidays. Snow blankets the city reflecting the Christmas lights which are everywhere. There are so many winter activities—skiing, snowboarding, snow mobiling, ice skating, and ice fishing on Lake of the Woods to mention the obvious. But there are others. We even have a snow sculpting contest that is breathtaking. Let me know if and when a winter visit is possible and I will make sure that your room and the adjoining one for Rebecca are available. Tell Rebecca that Josey would see to it that she is well entertained. They would have fun together—and so would we.

I miss you, too, Eric—our meals together and our outings. I miss knowing you are here in my house.
Affectionately,

Margie

* * *

Eric to Margie

We're coming for Christmas!! I purchased airline tickets today for Rebecca and me. Arriving Dec 19, staying for a week. I will rent a car at the airport. Will the roads be passable to Kenora? I look forward to seeing you again. Rebecca is anxious to meet you and Josey.

Affectionately,

Eric/Terry

* * *

Margie to Eric

So glad you will be here for Christmas. I'm eager to meet your daughter. Please don't bother to rent a car. I'll pick you up at the airport. Charlie says he give you a loaner for the week. Did I mention that Charlie, Nancy, and I have become close friends? (Thanks to you!) Josey has 100 things planned for Rebecca. There is an adorable cottage for sale on a lake near Kenora. Thought you might be interested in it as a far north getaway cabin. We'll take a look if you like. I can't wait to be with you again.
Lovingly,
Margie

Eric to Margie

The cabin is a great idea. A real possibility for the future. We'll check it out if it's still available.

Eric/Terry

* * *

Eric to Charlie

Hey Charlie,

I want to express to you and Nancy my gratitude for all the kindness you showed me. Charlie, you're the best boss a man could have! I miss our discussions (and sometimes disagreements) about the best way to handle a repair problem. I miss our "brew" time together after work and I certainly miss Nancy's great bag lunches as well as dinners at your home. Not only were you fair and honest in your dealings with me, but you were also incredibly generous.

I especially want to thank you for respecting my privacy—or rather secrecy. You never asked questions that would have put me on the spot, rather you shielded me from them. You believed in me and trusted me. I'm glad I could help out in the shop. In fact, I loved my job in Kenora.

My daughter and I will be visiting your little town for Christmas. I really want her to meet you. I hope we can all get together. I'm sure Margie will be contacting you to make arrangements.

Your friend and former employee,

Eric/Terry

* * *

Charlie to Eric

Hey!

Good to hear from you, buddy. Glad you are out of trouble and back together with family. I bet that little girl of yours is mighty happy to have her daddy again. I'm the one who should express gratitude. You helped me out when I was in a tight spot for lack of a mechanic. I have one now, but he's only part time and he's not "Terry." Don't know if I'll ever get used to calling you by another name. Yeah, I miss our after-work time, too. I still go over to the brewery for a beer now and then.

That's great news about your upcoming visit at Christmas. Nance is already planning the menu for a dinner party. I know Margie is excited about it. You know me, I always speak my mind, and I just want to say that you and Margie make a perfect couple. She really cares for you. Since you were here, she and Nance have become good friends and she has confided some things to my wife. Keep all that under your cap and I'll see you in December.

Charlie

P.S. The Ranchero is still purring like a kitten.

* * *

Karen to Meredith and Mark

My Sweet Children,

I know this is a busy time for you getting ready to open the lodge for the summer. That's why I'm using email instead of the phone so you can read it when you get a moment.

Bobby and I want you to know how proud we are of you for the way you managed the lodge last summer. You had some tough situations to deal with—the bear attack, the missing fisherman, the boating accident, the bear in camp at dinnertime. But the two of you handled it all with cool heads and warm hearts. Mark, I am truly amazed at your ability to dominate and communicate with bears. And you, Meredith, your instincts and investigative powers are astonishing. You make a brilliant couple.

That brings me to tell you that Bobby and I will not be at the lodge this summer. You two should move into our cabin. In the future we will make short, occasional visits, but for now we want to spend quality time with Jenny. She is involved in so many activities. I can't keep up with them all. In addition, we want to travel the world a bit. We're taking the grand tour of Europe this summer and a Caribbean cruise over the Christmas holidays. You are welcome to join us! If there is time between Jenny and the travels, I'd like to get back to the piano, do some professional accompanying or solo performances on a small scale. All this is to say that we have 100% confidence in you guys. We'll make sure you can always reach us if you need us, but I don't think you will. If you get weary of the vicissitudes of life and find love fading or slipping into the background, spend some time at the Poplar River outpost. It will renew your love of life and each other. It's magical! Lots and lots of love,

Mama

Chapter Seventeen
Naku

At first light Naku left his mother sleeping. More and more he was drawn away from her. Instinct was pulling him. He wanted to find his own food, to hear and understand the meanings of all the forest sounds and smells on his own. For some time now with great joy and confidence he had been feeling his independence. He had learned where and when to discover the vegetation he loved, he knew where to look for ground runners, longears, and other small creatures. He had been taught how to keep his claws and teeth sharp, how to mark territory, how to catch swimmers going through the rapids, and many other things.

"Yes, she has been a good instructor and provider of food. I will always remember her and all the meals she shared with me." Just then he remembered the fatty, meaty-tasting meal he and his mother enjoyed this past light cycle. "It was not far from the uprights' big nest, but even though we were aware of the uprights' presence in the little nests, she seemed to feel it was okay to lap up some of the food. And it was so good!" Thinking about the tasty stuff made Naku decide to go back there and have some more. Right now. By himself.

It didn't take him long to find his way. But the food was gone. The little nests were open. He stuck his head inside one of them. No uprights, no food. He didn't understand. What most confused him was not the absence of uprights or the lack of food, but the odor of wounded flesh, the flesh of one of his own kind. He raised his muzzle and sniffed vigorously. The scent he inhaled was compelling and he followed it. It led him into thick brush and beyond where dark spots of life's liquid dotted the forest floor.

"Something is wrong." Naku felt an imbalance in the forest around him and in his own spirit as he continued to follow the trail of the wounded. A strong smell of uprights lingered and mingled with the scent of the injured animal. The odor had grown strong and overpowering. Above him he heard the whirr of the roaring bird approaching the uprights' big nest. When he looked up to try to see the bird through the dense canopy, he spotted claw scratchings on the tree. He recognized the markings. He lowered his gaze. There at the base of the tree was what was left of Kuru. Kuru—esteemed, venerated and feared by all the denizens of the forest including himself, most especially himself. Out of respect he dared not approach the body. His nose told him all he needed to know. Kuru was dead. The uprights had been there. They were responsible. Naku sat down and waited beside the body of Kuru. He sat for quite a while.

As he sat a plethora of strange feelings ran rampant through his heart. Shock, fear, confusion, sadness, anger—feelings he had never experienced before. The great light reached the center of the sky and began its descent. Like the light, the odd sensations ebbed and in their place an awareness and calm determination formed in Naku's heart and mind.

"This is my forest now. I am sovereign here. I will be respected and admired by all the forest dwellers. I am Kuru now." He turned away from the body and loped to a nearby white pine. He stood on hind legs, stretched up as tall as he could, and dug his claws deep into the trunk drawing out the sap. He clawed and clawed, thereby saying clearly to all the forest and its creatures:

"I am Naku. This is my forest. Beware."

www.ingramcontent.com/pod-product-compliance
Lightning Source LLC
Chambersburg PA
CBHW052137170626
46812CB00004B/1474